FOREST OF LIES

ALEXIS FORREST MYSTERY
BOOK 4

KATE GABLE

COPYRIGHT

Copyright © 2024 by Byrd Books, LLC. All rights reserved.

Proofreader:

Renee Waring, Guardian Proofreading Services, https://www.facebook.com/GuardianProofreadingServices

Cover Design: Kate Gable

No part of this book may be reproduced in any form or by any electronic or mechanical means, including information storage and retrieval systems, without written permission from the author, except for the use of brief quotations in a book review.

This book is a word of fiction. Names, characters, places, and incidents are either products of the author's imagination or are used fictitiously. Any resemblance to actual persons, living or dead, events, or locales is entirely coincidental. The author acknowledges the trademarked status and trademark owners of various products referenced in this work of fiction, which have been used without permission. The publication/use of these trademarks is not authorized, associated with, or sponsored by the trademark owners.

Visit my website at www.kategable.com

BE THE FIRST TO KNOW ABOUT MY UPCOMING SALES, NEW RELEASES AND EXCLUSIVE GIVEAWAYS!

Want a Free book? Sign up for my Newsletter!

Sign up for my newsletter:
https://www.subscribepage.com/kategableviplist

Join my Facebook Group:
https://www.facebook.com/groups/
833851020557518

Bonus Points: Follow me on BookBub and Goodreads!

https://www.goodreads.com/author/show/21534224.Kate_Gable

ABOUT KATE GABLE

Kate Gable is a 3 time Silke Falchion award winner including Book of the Year. She loves a good mystery that is full of suspense. She grew up devouring psychological thrillers and crime novels as well as movies, tv shows and true crime.

Her favorite stories are the ones that are centered on families with lots of secrets and lies as well as many twists and turns. Her novels have elements of psychological suspense, thriller, mystery and romance.

Kate Gable lives near Palm Springs, CA with her husband, son, a dog and a cat. She has spent more than twenty years in Southern California and finds inspiration from its cities, canyons, deserts, and small mountain towns.

She graduated from University of Southern California with a Bachelor's degree in Mathematics. After pursuing graduate studies in mathematics, she switched gears and got her MA in Creative Writing and English from Western New Mexico University and her PhD in Education from Old Dominion University.

Writing has always been her passion and obsession. Kate is also a USA Today Bestselling author of romantic suspense under another pen name.

Write her here:

Kate@kategable.com

Check out her books here:

www.kategable.com

Sign up for my newsletter:
https://www.subscribepage.com/kategableviplist

Join my Facebook Group:
https://www.facebook.com/groups/833851020557518

Bonus Points: Follow me on BookBub and Goodreads!

https://www.bookbub.com/authors/kate-gable

https://www.goodreads.com/author/show/21534224.Kate_Gable

- amazon.com/Kate-Gable/e/B095XFCLL7
- facebook.com/KateGableAuthor
- bookbub.com/authors/kate-gable
- instagram.com/kategablebooks
- tiktok.com/@kategablebooks

ALSO BY KATE GABLE

Detective Kaitlyn Carr Psychological Mystery series
Girl Missing (Book 1)
Girl Lost (Book 2)
Girl Found (Book 3)
Girl Taken (Book 4)
Girl Forgotten (Book 5)
Gone Too Soon (Book 6)
Gone Forever (Book 7)
Whispers in the Sand (Book 8)

Girl Hidden (FREE Novella)

Detective Charlotte Pierce Psychological Mystery series
Last Breath
Nameless Girl

**Missing Lives
Girl in the Lake**

ABOUT FOREST OF LIES

Forensic psychologist and FBI agent Alexis Forrest returns in her most chilling case yet. Set against the backdrop of Broken Hill, the small New England town where she grew up, she now faces her darkest challenge: a fourteen-year-old boy doesn't show up to school after spending the night with his father and stepmother.

Meanwhile, Alexis receives a sinister note threatening her and her family from the serial killer who took her sister's life.

Together with her old flame and partner Mitch, a bookstore and coffee shop owner, Alexis embarks on a race against time to protect her loved ones and capture the predator who always seems to be one step ahead.

Amidst the chaos, Alexis grapples with haunting questions: Is the missing boy just a teenage runaway or a victim of the serial killer who haunts this area?

When a fire consumes her father's mobile home, Alexis finds herself in the path of the murderer who's been the source of her nightmares since she was a teen.

The only difference is that now she knows his name.

With a serial killer lurking, emboldened by the game of leaving mementos, Alexis's journey is more than a quest for justice; it's a fight to restore peace to herself and to the town of Broken Hill. Her path is fraught with challenges, but Alexis Forrest stands unwavering, determined to confront her demons and bring the murderer to justice, whatever the personal cost.

KILLER

I'm beginning to get bored, and bad things happen when I'm bored. I get unsettled, jumpy. I start looking for ways to keep myself entertained, and that rarely ends well for whoever I decide to be entertained by.

So the happy couple has reunited. How nice for them. The lights in the house went off fairly early last night. I can't help smirk to myself – Mitch will be in a good mood today, no doubt. So will Alexis. Now that she's closed her case, she can go back to her life. What a sweet, lovely ending for everyone involved.

My smirk turns to a scowl. What about me? I know she hasn't forgotten. I'm always there, a shadow hanging over her, darkening everything in her life the way I have for the past two decades. There's no shaking me. I will always be there.

Normally, it's enough to know that. It satisfies me. She knows I exist, knows I'm still out here, that I could take another life at any moment. I have that power. I always have. The power to control lives, to decide when it's time for one to end.

Let's be honest. Sometimes, a man needs a little excitement. He needs confirmation that he hasn't been forgotten. And with all her blissful, romantic nonsense going on, it's easy to imagine Alexis forgetting me for the time being.

No one forgets me. I will not be forgotten. I will not be disregarded.

It's only when a sharp, stinging pain erupts in my palms that I notice I've dug my nails in as far as I can without breaking the skin. There's a marching band blaring away in my head and the edges of my vision are starting to go red.

All work and no play make Jack a dull boy. Isn't that how the saying goes? I haven't had nearly enough playtime lately. That little game with Alexis was a fun diversion, but she put it behind her sooner than I expected. Busy looking for that so-called victim, the doctor's wife. Anybody could've told her the woman kidnapped herself, but then the public tends to want to believe the best about young, affluent homemakers. The type who portray themselves as saints, selfless, devoted to nothing but their families and their homes.

Forest of Lies

I'm the last person to be fooled by anything like that, since I know what it means to hide behind a mask. To need more than what the world sees fit to give me, more than it thinks I deserve.

It's well past time to remind Alexis I'm watching. Missing her. Craving the satisfaction of her panic. I need it like I need oxygen.

The frustration which literally moments ago threatened to overwhelm me eases and turns into something warm and pleasant. It's knowing she's happy right now, in the arms of the man she loves or at least cares for. As far as she's concerned, all is right with the world.

And here I am, about to ruin that. The sense of power is heavy, intoxicating. Like a drug, one I've become dependent on. No, more like a fine wine. I like that better. Something I can savor, roll around in my mouth, let it play on my senses. I only wish I could be here when she finds the gift I'm about to leave, but it would be too great a risk. We can't always have our cake and eat it, too.

I'll have to live on imagining how she'll react to the tube of red lipstick I retrieve from the glove box. At first, I planned on leaving my message on her car the way I did before — but a lightbulb goes on in my head, and a delicious shiver runs down my spine when another idea takes its place. I could kill two birds with one stone and leave the note on Mitch's truck, instead. So they'll both know she isn't the only one I'm following. That I am part of her life, whether she was aware of it or not. Always watching. Always aware.

My hands begin trembling with anticipation, but I steady them before pulling on a pair of latex gloves and retrieving a sheet of plain, blank paper. The blood red lipstick is bright and glaring against the stark whiteness as I scrawl my message in big, block letters.

I'm coming for you. But first, your mom.

Short and sweet, but more than enough to get her imagination going. Sometimes, what the imagination can come up with is more horrific than anything that can happen in reality.

It's still fully dark when I open my door. The air is so cold it takes my breath away, but I like it. It's invigorating. It reminds me I'm alive. I pull in a deep breath as I climb from the car, crossing the street to where Mitch parked in front of his house. She is up there, sleeping soundly I'm sure. Wrapped in the arms of her man. The man who thinks he's above all of this, outside of it. He has no idea I'm about to pull him in simply because I feel like it. My heart pounds with anticipation and satisfaction as I lift his wiper and tuck the note underneath it, the letters plain and clear so there's no missing them.

Forest of Lies

As an afterthought, I withdraw my pocket knife and plunge it into each tire. A little flourish, if you will. "I guess you'll be late for work today," I murmur, grinning.

I really would like to be here to watch their reaction, but it's too dangerous. If I want to keep playing my games, I need to control my impulses. Alexis is much too fun a playmate to bring this to an end quickly.

Just like her sister.

I wonder if Alexis is as strong a fighter as her sister was, too. When the time comes for us to get better acquainted – and it will – she'll put me through my paces the way Madeline did.

I hope she does. I truly do.

That always makes the inevitable ending that much sweeter.

1

BENJI

"I'm just saying. That part never made sense to me."

Pete rolled his eyes in a way that made Benji wish he had never said anything. "I'm telling you, it's really simple."

"How do you know?" Benji demanded. No matter how he raised his voice, there was no cutting through the general noise of the school cafeteria. "You didn't write the books. You didn't write the movies."

Another eye roll, this time followed by a groan. "I know because I go online and read what other people say, and everybody agrees." Pete dumped a couple of fries into a cup of ketchup before cramming them into his mouth. He didn't bother swallowing before he continued. "Gandalf turned into what Saruman was supposed to be. That's what he was saying when he told Aragon and them that he became Saruman."

"How could he become Saruman when Saruman still existed?" Benji took a single fry and swirled it in his ketchup.

Pete brushed dark hair away from his forehead, then set his food aside before folding his hands on the cafeteria table. Sometimes, being friends with Pete was like being in school all the time. He was a good friend, fun to hang out with even if they were pretty different in lots of ways. They had plenty of things in common, like *Lord of the Rings*. There weren't many people Benji felt comfortable talking about stuff like that with. Most of the kids in their grade were more into making TikToks or hanging out in the woods with beer or whatever else they could sneak out of their parents' houses.

Pete was cool because Pete never forced Benji into doing anything he didn't want to do. There was none of that pressure stuff. It was enough to hang out, watch movies, play games.

That didn't mean Benji liked feeling like he was in front of a teacher who was getting tired of trying to describe the same idea over and over. "Saruman got, like, twisted up," Pete explained. "He and Gandalf and the other wizards were sent to Middle Earth to, like, guide mankind in the right direction. But

Saruman ended up getting seduced or whatever by Sauron and all the power he thought he'd end up with."

"I know. I saw the movies."

"That's what he was trying to say. He was doing what Saruman was supposed to do, so that's why he said he was Saruman." Pete leaned in a little, and Benji noticed the way his cheeks got redder and his eyes got brighter. He was that into the topic. "Saruman was always jealous that people liked Gandalf better. And that's always the person who is easiest to, like, twist up. Sauron used his ego against him. Gandalf had to take his place."

Benji thought it over while chewing another fry. It made sense. "Why can't they just come out and explain it like that?" he wondered.

Pete snickered, then picked up his second slice of pizza. "Because then you wouldn't be able to go on online and talk with people about theories and stuff. That's half the fun."

Benji didn't see it that way. If he was watching a movie to have fun, he didn't want to have to basically do homework afterward so all of it would make sense. But Pete was like that. He liked thinking about things, coming up with reasons why characters acted like they did, looking into the backgrounds and legends and stuff. "I was thinking about reading the books sometime."

"You totally should, but they're way different from the movies in a lot of ways," Pete advised. "I mean, you know, I think it's the best series that was ever made, but sometimes all the action scenes took away from the characters and the story. Like, there's a lot more about hobbits than you see on-screen."

"Maybe they put all that into the *Hobbit* movies."

Pete scoffed. "I'm going to pretend you didn't just mention them, since we're at school and I don't need to get detention for hitting you with my tray."

It always made Benji laugh, getting Pete worked up over the *Hobbit* movies. He liked *Lord of the Rings*, but Pete was a super fan. He kind of made it his whole personality.

And Benji had a feeling he knew why. It was something he would never say out loud to his best friend– he didn't want to insult him or hurt his feelings or anything like that. And they were close, sure, but that didn't mean they sat around and talked about their feelings the way girls did. It was okay for them to spend all their time talking about Middle Earth and Mordor and all that, but that didn't mean they were going to break out a tissue box and cry over stuff.

Forest of Lies

"You wanna come over this weekend?" Benji suggested. "We could watch the extended director's cut of *Return of the King*." The last time they tried, they had been interrupted. Life at Pete's house wasn't as peaceful as Benji's – in fact, Benji never knew life could be any other way until he and Pete became friends. Benji's dad was a lawyer, and all he had ever known was comfort and space. His house was a lot bigger and more comfortable than Pete's, and there were always his favorite snacks around. He didn't have chores, since there was a housekeeper to clean up and a whole team of guys who did the lawn and landscaping in warm weather. All his parents ever really asked was that he keep his grades up and not get into any trouble, so life was pretty good.

It wasn't the same for Pete, and it never had been. His dad owned a bar, so it wasn't like they were poor or anything, but it wasn't the same as the kind of money a lawyer made.

Now, things were worse for him. That was why Benji made it a point to ask his friend over. "You could spend the night," he offered when Pete frowned. "Sunday morning, my mom always makes pancakes and stuff."

"That sounds good." But Pete was still frowning, and he spoke softly enough that Benji had to lean closer to hear over the other voices around them. "I don't know if I can come, though."

"Why not?"

"Because Mom wants me around. She's been working all these night shifts at the hospital, but this weekend she's got Saturday free. So she was hoping I would hang around and we could do stuff together or whatever."

"That's cool, though," Benji offered. "Lots of people have parents who don't want to even look at them most of the time."

When Pete flinched, Benji knew he'd made a mistake. It was a shame there was no way to go back in time and erase something stupid like that.

Pete then snorted before he took an angry bite of his pizza. "At least I have one parent who still cares," he muttered, narrowing his eyes and making Benji wish again that he hadn't said something so stupid.

2

BENJI

"How's it going with your parents?" It was weird, asking a question like that, but it was obvious Pete wasn't in the mood to talk about *Lord of the Rings* anymore. He was angry, frowning down at his food. Benji had never wished harder that he had kept his mouth shut.

"It's so nasty," he finally muttered, shaking his head. "You see stuff like this on TV, in movies. There's lots of kids in school whose parents have gotten divorced. But you don't know how gross and awful things can get until you see it and hear it yourself. Like, I know they're grown-ups or whatever and they have stuff going on that they never told me about. Just like I have stuff I don't tell them about. But I really thought they had it together. Do you know what I mean? Other kids' parents, you see them and they're having those quiet fights they think nobody else notices, or they get all weird and fake when they're trying to cover something up. But it wasn't like that with them. I didn't think it was, anyway."

As much as Benji didn't really want to talk about this, it was kind of obvious Pete needed to. Benji was his closest friend – who else was he going to talk to about it? And most of the time, Benji tried to avoid bringing it up because he didn't want to make things awkward. Too late now.

He cleared his throat and hoped he wouldn't say the wrong thing. "Yeah, well, your mom didn't know what your dad was doing. She was just as surprised as you were, I guess." The way Pete told it, it was one of those situations where his mom was totally clueless and figured her husband worked long hours because he owned his own business and had lots of work to do. One night, she got off a shift at the hospital where she worked as a nurse and thought she would go to the bar to say hi. She ended up finding Pete's dad in his office with one of his bartenders, and they weren't talking about business. Since then, they had been fighting over a divorce, going back and forth. As much as Pete tried to hide his feelings, it was clear he was miserable about it.

When Benji tried to imagine the same thing with his parents, he couldn't make the picture come up in his mind. His mom and dad had always been in love – kinda gross, but it was the truth. He would sometimes walk into the kitchen and see them dancing together, and he had walked in on them kissing more times than he wanted to remember. Hearing about Pete's family took some of the grossness out of the memories. He felt a little safer, more secure, knowing his parents still loved each other and his world wouldn't get totally shaken up like his friend's had.

"Sometimes, I hear her crying when she thinks I'm asleep." There was anger in Pete's voice when he said it. He was probably thinking about his dad, blaming him for all of it.

"That's rough," Benji mused. What was the right thing to say? Was there anything he could say to make it better? Probably not.

"I just hate that he gets to go off and live his life however he wants to while she's crying at night and trying to figure out how to make things work with him gone."

"That sucks." Especially since Pete's mom was a nice lady. Pretty, too. Even though she worked crazy hours, she always looked nice. *She takes care of herself*, his mom would say, and she was right. He would never say it out loud to Pete, but Benji figured his dad had to be pretty stupid to cheat on somebody like Becky McLintock.

Benji leaned in, craning his neck to catch Pete's eye when he wouldn't look up from his tray. "Hey. It doesn't have to be all bad. Once they get their stuff worked out, you get two Christmases. That's pretty cool, right?"

He was trying to be a good friend the only way he knew how, but his weak joke only made Pete's frown deepen. "Yeah, right," he muttered. "I can barely get him to remember my birthday. Forget Christmas. Besides," he added with a sneer, "it's not like I would want to spend Christmas with her."

It was always this way whenever Pete mentioned the girl his dad was cheating with. Pete hated her, and Benji figured he'd feel the same way if he was in his friend's place. She had to know Pete's dad was married, but that didn't stop her. It didn't stop him, either.

Again, the image of his parents dancing in the kitchen popped up in Benji's head, and he almost felt bad for gagging and rolling his eyes whenever he caught them that way. "Yeah, but they probably won't stay together." He kept to himself the conversation he'd overheard where his mom had predicted their relationship wouldn't last the time it took for the divorce to finalize. Mr. McLintock was what his mom called a handsome devil, and he had a wandering eye.

Forest of Lies

"I don't know. Last time I saw him, it sounded pretty serious between him and Brittany." Pete slumped in the plastic chair and looked miserable.

"You didn't tell me that."

"I didn't want to talk about it," Pete explained with a shrug. "It's so gross. They're talking about maybe getting married once the divorce is finalized."

"That sucks, man. I'm sorry."

"I just don't get it," Pete sighed. "He thinks we're gonna be a family or something. I almost laughed in his face. A family? What does that mean, anyway? We were a family. We were supposed to be normal. I was supposed to have parents who wanted to be married to each other."

"My mom always tells me I'll understand one day, when I'm older," Benji told him.

"I'll never understand," Pete murmured, shaking his head until his dark hair flopped over his forehead. "Not ever. All that lying. Sneaking around and stuff. I mean, for fourteen years my dad's been telling me to keep my promises and be honest, and how a man owns up to his mistakes and all that stuff. But there he was, lying to both of our faces all that time. I'm supposed to believe anything he ever said?"

Now Benji wished more than ever that he had never gotten them on the topic, since Pete looked and sounded totally miserable. "You know, my dad says the same stuff to me, too," he offered, feeling awkward. "So it must be true, right?"

"I guess so," Pete agreed. "Your dad's an honest guy."

Benji snickered. "Okay, hold up. He's still a lawyer." At least that made Pete laugh.

Then his eyes lit up. "Hey. Maybe you can come over today after school. We still have that Assassin's Creed game we saved the last time you came over."

"Sure, that sounds good," Benji agreed. "I'll call my mom, but she won't mind."

"Cool." Still, another frown passed over his friend's face as they started getting their stuff together before the end of the period. "And maybe with you around, my mom won't talk about the child bride." Pete made quotation marks with his fingers, then rolled his eyes. "It makes me feel sick. Brittany is fifteen years younger than him. She's closer to my age than his."

It did sound pretty gross when Pete put it that way. "Is she nice?"

"How would I know? I barely ever see her, and when I do, she acts like I'm too much of a pain in the ass to bother with. And with all the custody stuff

Forest of Lies

and whatever, it's awkward for them to work out visitation." All of a sudden, his head snapped up. "What if they want me to live with them after they're married? That would be the worst."

"I think the judge will ask you who you want to live with once it's time to work that stuff out." Secretly, Benji had asked his dad about it when all of this first started. He was curious, and worried about his friend.

Pete barked out a laugh. "Oh, I don't even have to think about it. I can either live with my dad and some girl who's practically my age who ignores me, or I can live with my mom who actually cares."

"You would choose her?"

"I wouldn't even think about it. Besides, I'm not leaving her." Deep down inside, Benji knew there would be a time when he'd have to leave his mom, the way everybody had to leave their mom eventually. But that wouldn't be for a long time, so he settled for awkwardly patting his friend's shoulder after they threw out their trash. "Well, you don't have to worry about that right now. You should be more worried about Mr. Cooper's art history exam on Friday."

That was all it took to change the subject, and Benji was glad. Pete was a good friend. It sucked that he was going through all this because his parents couldn't get it together.

They made plans to meet up at Pete's locker after last bell, then parted ways outside the cafeteria. Benji was glad to see Pete grinning as he walked away.

3

ALEXIS

I'm in shock. There's still part of my brain capable of conscious thought, and it's clear that I'm in shock as I stare at the ugly message left on Mitch's truck.

"What is this?" Mitch reaches for the paper under his wiper, where the dark red letters scream out against paper as stark as fresh snow.

That's all it takes to shake me out of my stunned silence. "No!" I bark, pulling him back. "Don't touch it. There could be fingerprints. We have to be careful."

Funny, thinking about being careful at a time like this. Is there any way to be careful when there's someone out there watching your every move while you go through life without a clue where they are or what they'll do next?

His head snaps back and forth as he looks around. "Where is he? Where are you?" he demands, raising his voice to an angry shout.

"He's probably gone by now," I decide, looking up and down the street. I hope he is, anyway. I hope he isn't watching us unravel.

Mitch leans in closer to the note to get a better look. "It's not paint," he decides, even sniffing the paper. "But it doesn't look like ink."

"Lipstick," I realize. "It's just lipstick. But how did he… where is he?…" The part of my brain that is still thinking clearly feels sorry for Mitch, who has finally been thrown headfirst into my mess. Until now, he's had the luxury of existing outside of it, maybe brushing up against it every so often, but still removed from the worst of it. Now here we are, and there's no way he isn't involved.

"Do me a favor." I'm already backing away, toward the house. "Go inside and get a baggie so we can package up the note." Meanwhile, I pull my cell from my pocket with a shaking hand. My teeth are chattering, and it's not from the cold. *Please, let this be him messing with me. Please, let it all be a sick joke.* I don't know what I would do if it weren't. I can't bring myself to imagine it being any different.

"Answer, answer," I whisper, rocking from my heels to the balls of my feet. Her phone does not want to comply–nothing but the sound of ringing fills my ear until frustrated tears fill my eyes.

Mitch is on his way out the door with a baggie in hand, and we almost collide on the steps before I push my way past him. "What are you doing?" he calls out, following me through the house.

"I'm getting my keys. She's not answering her phone." My voice is shaking almost as hard as my body while I fumble through putting on my coat and grabbing my purse.

"You're not going to drive." He's already punching his fists through his sleeves and pulling on his hat. "Not the way you are right now."

"Why wouldn't she answer? Why?" It's a silly question. I know very well all the various reasons why she might not answer the phone now that this maniac has set his sights on her. But has he? I have never so wished to find out someone is messing with my head. *Please, let that be the case. Please, let her be okay.*

I try again to call her on my way out the door, but I get no further than I did before. All I hear is her chipper greeting and the invitation to leave a voicemail. "Mom, please, call me the second you get this." It doesn't occur to me until after I've ended the call that she might take it the wrong way and assume there's something wrong with me. Right now she can do that, since the sooner she calls me, the better. If she thinks I'm in trouble, she'll be more inclined to call me back right away. I wouldn't normally want to worry her, but this is an extreme circumstance. He's not playing around anymore. That much is obvious. This time, he's gone right for the jugular.

I bag the note and tuck it into my purse before dropping into the passenger seat of my Corolla, which Mitch is already warming up. As soon as I'm belted in he takes off for Mom's, his jaw tight, his eyes narrowed.

"He's not satisfied." I'm rocking in my seat, ugly images flashing through my head. Why won't this car go faster?

"What do you mean?" Mitch asks.

"It wasn't enough just to mess with me the way he did before." I still shudder when I remember the wild goose chase he sent me on, leaving a note on my car to let me know he was watching, setting up an innocent man to take the fall. He was willing to paw through garbage to pull out a receipt if it meant watching me chase my tail. I can put nothing past him.

"And last time, nothing came out of it," he reminds me in a strained voice. I'm not fooled. He's just as worried as I am. He's only trying to stay calm and

Forest of Lies

level headed for my sake. Part of me wants to tell him not to waste his time, that nothing is going to make me feel better until I am with Mom and I know she's safe.

He wouldn't go this far, would he? I can't believe it. "If he wants me, let him mess with me," I whisper, my teeth clenched while bitter tears well in my eyes. "He can't do this to her."

"And you don't know for sure yet whether he did anything or not." As always, Mitch is the voice of reason. I appreciate it, but there's still part of me that knows he doesn't get it. He has never been through what my family has suffered. He doesn't know the horror of losing someone he loves in such a violent, cruel way. And he has certainly never been taunted by the killer years later.

"You're not going to get there any faster that way." It's only when Mitch says it that I realize I'm jamming my right foot against the floorboards like that's going to do anything to make the car go faster. Why does she have to live so far away from Mitch? Why are there so many cars on the road at this time of the morning? I want to scream and am barely able to stop myself by grinding my teeth hard. I don't want to upset him, even though it feels like my entire world is falling apart and there's nothing I can do to stop it.

That's not quite true. There is one thing I can do to prepare for the worst. This time, rather than pulling up Mom's contact, I pull up the number for Captain Felch's desk. He answers right away, and I could weep with relief when he does. "We have a problem," I blurt out right away.

"Since when is that new?" he asks with a sigh.

"I'm serious!" I shout, panic shimmering on the edge of my voice. "There was a note on Mitch's truck. Something about coming for me, but first going for my mom. He actually threatened my mother!"

"All right. Breathe. Where are you?" he asks. "Tell me you aren't driving."

"Mitch is," I tell him before releasing a whimper. Here I am, a big, bad FBI agent, and I'm whimpering with fear and dread like a child. When it comes to our mothers, I guess we're all children in a way. Especially when we feel entirely helpless. "What if he hurt her? What if he—"

"And what if this is nothing more than another trick?" he counters. "It could be. He wants to remind you he's around. He wants to get under your skin."

"Congratulations to him, then," I announce. "He managed to do that."

Forest of Lies

"Breathe," he urges. "I need you to breathe for me. I'll see if we have any cars in the area and send them straight to her."

"We're only a few minutes away," I announce in relief. "We'll make it to her before they will." *Please, don't let us need them. Please, please, anything but this.* I can't imagine life without her. It amazes me to think of the years that passed in near silence as she dealt with her demons and I focused everything I had on my career. We would go months at a time without talking. It seems unthinkable now, and it would be too cruel to take her away after we just found each other again.

"Do you want me to stay on the phone with you?" the captain asks in a voice heavy with concern.

"No—but thanks. I'll … " My throat closes up, but somehow I push through. "I will call you if I need you."

"Keep me posted, either way." He sounds grim, like he's dreading this the way I am. But he doesn't know. He can't possibly understand. If only I had found this guy before now. If only I had seen him for who he was when we met that day at the boarding school, when I dismissed him as nothing more than a maintenance man who happened to be nearby so I could get directions. *Way to go, Agent Forrest. Letting the bad guy slip through your fingers.*

I'm sure wherever he is, Tyler Mahoney is having a nice laugh at my expense.

I can only hope that's all it is as we turn the corner and roll down Mom's block, approaching the familiar Victorian.

4

BENJI

"Sorry the place is kinda messy." Pete grimaced over his shoulder after he unlocked the front door to the little ranch house he used to share with both parents and now only shared with his mom.

Right away, Benji shivered once he was out of his coat. He considered keeping it on, but he didn't want to be rude. He noticed the way Pete went straight to his room and came out with a hoodie which he pulled over his long sleeve t-shirt. Whenever he passed a window, Benji could feel the draft coming through. The heater hummed, though, and there was warm air coming from the vents. He wondered vaguely how much money it cost to keep this place as chilly as it was, then realized he didn't have the first idea what it cost to keep his own house warm and comfortable. It had to be three times the size of

Pete's, with five bedrooms plus an office for his dad and a hobby room for his mom. They even had a maid who came every week. The whole place was always clean and welcoming.

It wasn't that Pete's house was dirty, exactly, but it was cluttered. Everywhere he turned, something was stashed or stacked. Mail, magazines, bills. Plenty of bills. There were two trash bags sitting next to the back door in the kitchen—when Pete caught Benji glancing toward them while he grabbed sodas from the fridge, he rolled his eyes. "His stuff." That was all the explanation he received, and all the explanation he needed. "Clothes, mostly." There was also an ironing board in the kitchen and a stack of nurse's scrubs folded up at one end.

The sink was full of dishes, and it made Benji think of how good he had it. It wasn't like he felt sorry for Pete or anything like that—except when it came to all the stuff with his parents, of course. But he didn't pity his friend. He wasn't totally clueless.

His mom's bedroom door was closed, but her car was outside. "She worked the night shift again," Pete explained in a quiet voice as he started unloading the dishwasher. "Let me just do this real quick, then we can go to my room."

Benji winced to himself when he remembered being annoyed the last time Margaret, the housekeeper, was sick and his mom asked him to unload the dishwasher. Here Pete was, doing it himself, without being asked, all so he could take a little weight off his mom's shoulders.

"I'll help you," Benji offered, and Pete patiently explained where everything went while he loaded the pots and plates from the sink into the dishwasher. It looked old, so old it was a surprise the thing worked. When Pete started it up, Benji wondered if the noise would wake Mrs. McLintock even though they had tried so hard to be quiet.

Every time Benji visited, he understood why Pete so rarely had him over. He was a little embarrassed by his house, and all the clutter. The old-fashioned shag carpeting needed a good vacuuming, and there was dust on just about every surface where there wasn't clutter covering it. Benji guessed it had to seem like a pretty big shift, visiting a big house where someone was paid to keep it clean and fresh. Maybe Pete compared it to his own house. Maybe he remembered Benji's big, open house and felt embarrassed even though Benji knew it was all because Mrs. McLintock worked crazier hours than normal now that she had legal bills on top of everything else.

Once they finished, they retreated to Pete's room. He kept it pretty neat, which helped make the small space feel more livable. He kicked off his sneakers and Benji did the same before they dropped onto the foot of the bed to play on the Xbox Pete had gotten two Christmases earlier, back when life was normal.

They weren't five minutes into their game when the door to the other bedroom opened. "Pete?" Benji recognized the voice of Becky McClintock and sat up a little straighter before he could help it.

"In my room," Pete called out. "Benji's here. We're just hanging out."

"Oh, I thought I heard two sets of footsteps." Becky appeared in the doorway, giving them both a sleepy grin as she wrapped a thick cardigan around her thin body. "Hi, Benji. How are you?"

Becky wasn't like the other moms. When she asked that question, it seemed like she actually wanted to know the answer. Adults were always asking that, but it rarely seemed like they listened to the answer. It was just something they said to each other. Small talk. "I'm good, thanks."

"Hungry?" she asked. "I can fix you something to eat."

Then she ran a hand over her dark hair and frowned. "I have to clean up the kitchen first."

"Don't worry about it," Pete told her, pausing the game to look at her. "We took care of it."

Her face glowed when she smiled, warming Benji from head to toe. "I'm about to do something very

Forest of Lies

embarrassing," she announced, entering the room. "Benji, you might want to look away."

No matter how Pete squirmed, he couldn't avoid the big, smacking kiss his mother delivered on his cheek. "Mom..." he grumbled, rolling his eyes.

Benji's heart almost stopped when Becky turned toward him. "You, too," she announced, turning his face to the side and placing a soft peck that made his face go warm and his insides even warmer. He would most definitely not have done something stupid like cheat on her the way Mr. McClintock had. What an idiot. Sure, she worked a lot, but even then she was kind and sweet.

And really, really pretty. It had been about a year since Benji first noticed her that way, around the time he turned thirteen. It wasn't like he thought anything would happen. He wasn't stupid. That didn't keep him from thinking about her all the time. Wishing there were something he could do to make her life better. Easier. It didn't seem fair that some people lived life on easy mode while other people fought just to get by. Becky worked all the time, picking up any shift she could no matter how long it ran or when she had last worked. It just didn't matter. She needed the money. And that was before her husband walked out like the idiot he was.

"If I ever find a girl like her, I'll never look at anybody else," he told himself, as Becky left them alone again.

Through the open door, he could hear her humming to herself in the kitchen.

"That's one thing that would never happen if I lived with Dad," Pete predicted as he went back to the game.

"What are you talking about?"

"You're not going to see Brittany offering to make dinner for us." He even gagged a little. "I hate saying her name."

"Then don't say it," Benji suggested, which only got Pete rolling his eyes again.

"Thanks, genius." Pete elbowed him and Benji elbowed him back, and they tussled a little before returning to the game. At least Pete was smiling and not thinking about his dad or Brittany anymore.

At least, that was what Benji thought before Pete frowned again. "I wish I could find a way to get them back together. He's a liar and a cheat, but life was better when they were together. For all of us."

Pete's dad might not have seen things the same way. Benji kept that thought to himself.

5

BENJI

It was turning into a weird day.

Where are you? Home sick? Usually, Pete would text if he stayed home so Benji would know. They only had Art class together toward the end of the day. Usually, though, they would see each other in the hall between classes or at each other's lockers. Benji had assumed they missed each other and that was it, since he hadn't heard anything from his friend or seen him around.

When it came time for lunch and Pete never joined him, that was when Benji got a little worried. Not very. People got sick all the time. Maybe it hit him overnight out of nowhere – that happened sometimes. One of those random bugs that could make you sure you were dying, that would make you so sick you could forget ever being well. Benji worried for a second that he might end up getting sick, too. He had only been at Pete's the day before. He felt fine, but Pete seemed like he felt fine yesterday.

By the time he got home later that afternoon, Benji still felt fine. "I'm home!" he called out from the mudroom, where he kicked off his shoes and left his coat and hat before continuing through the kitchen.

"How was your day?" his mom asked. She was in her workout clothes, touching a towel to her face and neck and chugging a big bottle of water.

"It was okay," he told her with a shrug. "Pete was out."

"Oh, that's a shame. I hope he's feeling okay tomorrow." She slid him a look he recognized right away. "Did that mean eating lunch by yourself?"

He heard the sympathy in the question and it made him feel like a loser. He knew his parents would rather have a son who played hockey like all the other guys his age, or maybe soccer or something. He was completely uncoordinated and would always rather have a book in his hands than a hockey stick or a ball. "It didn't matter. I'm gonna make a peanut butter and jelly. I'm starving."

"Have a yogurt and an apple, instead," his mother urged, already reaching for one in the fridge. "I'm making paella for dinner. I don't want you to spoil your appetite."

Pete would never believe it, but there were times when Benji wished his mom could be more like Pete's mom. In some ways that was weird, since he kind of had a crush on Mrs. McClintock. But she was just more ... normal. She didn't make things like paella for dinner. The night before, they'd had spaghetti and meat sauce with garlic bread that was really plain store-bought white bread with butter and garlic powder on top, popped in the oven for a few minutes. And it was delicious. Things didn't always have to be all fancy to be good. He kept his thoughts to himself and took his snack up to his room to start on his homework.

"Margaret left your laundry on the foot of your bed," his mom called out, which meant he had to put everything away once he got up there. It was sort of their compromise. When he was younger, he didn't mind his mom or anybody else going into his dresser to put things away. Now, it felt weird even though he wasn't hiding anything. He didn't want anybody going through his personal stuff.

He was in the middle of stacking sweaters in his closet when he barely caught the sound of his phone buzzing, still tucked in his backpack. He managed to reach it before the call cut off, but he hesitated before answering. It was an unfamiliar number with a local area code.

"Hello?" he asked, figuring it had to be a wrong number. He was too young for the spam calls his parents got all the time.

It wasn't a spam call, and it wasn't a wrong number. "Is this Benji?" a woman asked in a shaky voice. A little breathless, too. "This is Mrs. McClintock."

His heart started beating faster, since she had never called him before and it sounded like she was upset. "Yeah, it's Benji. What's wrong?"

"Is Pete with you?"

"No."

She let out a soft whimper before asking, "Did you see him today?"

A sick feeling started to stir in the pit of his stomach. The hair on the back of his neck rose as he sat on the foot of his bed, ignoring the laundry still waiting there. "No. I figured he was sick."

"Did he call you or text you at all? Have you seen anything from him online?"

"No." His throat was getting tight. It was harder to breathe. "You mean he didn't stay home sick?"

"Oh, I don't know!" It sounded like she might be crying or trying not to cry. "I'm sorry. I don't want to yell, but I don't know what to do. I was still at work when it was time to leave for school, so it made sense that he wasn't here when I got home this morning. But I just got up, and he wasn't home, and I realized I had no idea whether he was even here last night. After I went to work, I mean. I called the school, and they told me he was absent. But why would he be?"

That was what Benji wanted to know. All kinds of ugly thoughts ran through his head, the sort of stuff he saw on *Dateline* and shows like that. Kids who vanished while walking to school, or after they got snatched from their houses in the middle of the night. Pete had said once or twice that he didn't like being home all alone in the middle of the night while his mom worked at the hospital, and now the worries Benji had brushed off at the time came rushing back. Maybe there was a reason for him to be worried.

Or maybe it was something stupid that they would laugh about later. "Maybe he's at his dad's?" he asked. It was sort of uncomfortable mentioning Mr. McClintock, but it made sense. Where else would he be?

The soft sob he heard answered the question before she spoke. "I already called him. He hasn't seen Pete."

"Oh." His heart was sinking further by the second. This wasn't like Pete. Some kids, maybe—there would be stories around school now and then about kids who decided to run away. Sometimes, they didn't really want to run for good. They only wanted to prove a point, like their parents couldn't control them or something. Or they would go out and spend the night someplace and not bother telling their parents. Dumb stuff like that.

That wasn't Pete. All he ever wanted was to make life easier for his mom, not harder.

"Do you have any idea where he might be? Someplace you guys talked about, maybe? I don't know, someplace you hang out that I don't know about? I swear, you wouldn't get into any trouble if you told me about it. I wouldn't tell anybody. Only please, if Pete could be there ... "

"Honest, Mrs. McClintock, there's no place like that." It was weird, but he felt sorry for having to ruin her hopes. He didn't have any way to make her feel better or calm her down. "I'm sorry," he offered. "Like I said, I figured Pete was just sick today. He doesn't skip school, and we don't have any place where we hang out except for our houses, together."

"I know. I know, you're both good boys." She sniffled loudly and blew her nose. "Where could he be?"

"Do you want me to come over or something?" he suggested. "Maybe we could look for him."

Forest of Lies

"No, but thank you," she replied in a tearful voice. "I'm going to call the police and let them do the looking around."

The police. His best friend was missing and the police were going to look for him.

It was definitely turning out to be a weird day.

6

ALEXIS

"Mom?" It's almost a scream, but I can't help it. There is no chance of quieting myself, or of quieting the panic raging in my head as I burst through the front door to find a quiet house. "Mom! Where are you?"

"I'll check the garage," Mitch offers before doubling back down the front steps. He's already halfway around the house, trudging through old snow that's been frozen over by layers of ice. Dad's little workshop was out there. I can't imagine why she would've gone there, but we can't make any assumptions now.

The house is quiet, chilly as always thanks to the drafty windows. It feels colder than ever, the kind of cold that seeps into a person's bones and won't relinquish its hold even in the presence of a fire. I'm freezing to the point where my teeth are chattering, but that could also be the result of mind bending panic. "Mom! Answer me!" I bark, but the only response I receive is the echo of my own voice.

Her car is in the driveway. She has to be around here somewhere. I refuse to believe otherwise. I run blindly from room to room – what do I expect to find? Some clue. Some hint. Something, anything. I would accept some sort of accident here around the house, so long as it meant we could get her help.

Mitch opens the storm door, stomping his feet on the welcome mat to dislodge any ice from his boots before entering. He shakes his head, though he didn't need to. I see everything written across his face. "There's no sign of her out there. No footprints other than my own."

"Oh, Mitch … " I realize I'm swaying, maybe about to fall over, but I catch myself in time. I can't do that. I don't have that luxury. She might need help, and I can't help her if I succumb to fear.

Rather than drop to my knees, I try again to reach her on the phone. *Please, please, pick up.* I hear the phone ring in my ear, the sound is soon followed by a familiar buzzing. Mitch and I meet each other's gazes before he starts looking around, searching for the device.

"Oh, no," he groans from the front parlor, where Mom's phone is plugged into a charger next to the sofa.

"She wouldn't have gone out without her phone," I whisper, letting my hand fall to my side with my phone still clutched in it.

"What about the basement? I'll check down there. She might have fallen down the stairs." He's already on his way, leaving me with nothing to do but stare up the stairs leading to the second floor.

Incredible that I would hesitate even now. I haven't been up there since I came home. I've avoided it like I would avoid the plague, going out of my way to keep from even looking at the stairs sometimes. There's too much up there that I don't want to revisit.

Yet here I am, gripping the banister, dashing up before I can stop myself. "Mom? Are you in here?" I call out, flinging open the door to her bedroom, where everything is so familiar I might break down crying if I weren't so busy trying not to lose my grip. Everything is so much the same. Just like I remembered it. Considering everything she changed downstairs, you would think she would have renovated the bedroom she once shared with Dad. All she's done is replace the bed, which makes sense seeing as how so many years have passed. The time would have come to replace it, anyway. But the walls are the same, along with the rest of the furniture – heavy, old-fashioned, passed down from her parents.

Get it together. Furnishings aside, she is not here, nor is she in the spacious bathroom Maddie and I were forbidden from using except in an emergency. We had our own bathroom, which I now check, noting its pristine condition. I wonder when it was last used, if Mom ever uses it at all.

She wouldn't be in my room, would she? Or Maddie's, for that matter. Part of me can easily imagine her coming up here, wallowing in memories for a while. It's like ripping off a Band-Aid, getting it over with all at once. I throw open my old bedroom door and am startled to find cardboard boxes stacked everywhere, including on the bed. There's barely room to get the door open all the way.

All that's left is Maddie's room. Now I wish I had pulled myself together enough to check it out before today. It would have been hard enough then, without the prospect of my mother missing – or worse.

Then again, maybe this is better, because there's no chance for me to process the time capsule my sister's room has become. Everything's faded, no longer nearly as vibrant as it was when Maddie called it her own. Mom took the curtains from the windows, but that's the only difference.

I descend the stairs on shaking legs, gripping the banister for dear life. Mitch stands in front of them, breathing hard, his eyes darting over my face. He's looking for answers. I wish I had some to give him. "She's gone."

"All right, let's think." He runs both of his hands through his hair before taking me by the arms like he's trying to hold me together. "She could've taken a walk."

"Without her phone?"

"Stranger things have happened."

I want so much for it to be true, but the implications of that note go way beyond the message itself. "He hasn't only been following me around when I go to work," I whisper. Mitch blurs in front of me thanks to the tears I can't suppress. "He's been following me all over the place. He knows where you live. He knows what car you drive. Who's to say he hasn't followed me here a dozen times? He knows where she lives. There is nothing stopping him from luring her out somehow and … "

"You can't let yourself think that way."

"I have to!" I shout, making his head snap back in surprise before I force myself to take a breath. "I'm sorry. I don't mean to yell at you. I'm just … " Emotion cuts off anything else I was about to say, and Mitch pulls me in close, holding me tight. What am I going to do? How am I going to tell Dad?

Forest of Lies

"We're going to take this one step at a time," Mitch decides before releasing me. "You're going to call the captain and you're going to tell him what happened, and we're going to find her."

He's right. There are procedures to be followed at times like this. My world is spinning, and my heart is pounding, and I could be sick at any moment, but that doesn't mean I can afford to forget everything I know.

"What if ... " That's all I can manage to get out, staring into Mitch's troubled eyes while tears roll down my cheeks. "What if he ... ?"

The sudden opening of the storm door makes us both jump. "What goes on around here? What are you doing here at this hour of the morning?" Mom demands, huffing and puffing, her face red, her body wrapped in so many layers of clothes I might not have recognized her if we'd passed on the street.

"Mom?" It's like I'm watching a miracle come true as I stagger across the front hall and throw my arms around her before she's had time to take off her coat. It's her. She's here. My mom. Her concerned questions are silenced by my uncontrollable sobs.

"Honey! What happened?" She pats my back and strokes my hair and I can't let her go, I just can't. I couldn't unwind my arms from around her for all the money in the world.

"I can't breathe!" she finally gasps, laughing. "Will somebody please tell me what this is all about?"

"I'm sorry." I run my hands under my eyes after finally forcing myself to let her go. She brushes hair back from my face and studies me, concerned. Normally I'd gently stop her but right now, I'm too glad she's safe to make a fuss. "I didn't mean to scare you. It's just that … "

"What?" she demands, placing her hands on her hips when I can't find the words. She looks at Mitch, blowing out a frustrated sigh. "Somebody, fess up, or I'm going to go bonkers."

"We don't mean to worry you." He approaches me from behind and places his hands on my shoulders, squeezing gently. I lean back, resting against his broad chest, grateful as always for his calming presence. "But we woke up this morning to find a note on my truck. A threatening one. I'm sorry to say it, but the threat was directed at you."

"Me?" Mom whispers, and like magic the color drains from her face. Though she's in the house now and still wrapped in multiple layers, she wraps her arms around herself and shivers. "What kind of note? Who wrote it?"

"We don't know for sure," Mitch tells her. "Though we have an idea."

Forest of Lies

"And what is this idea?" There's anxiety in the question, and it breaks my heart. She has already been through so much. Losing her daughter in the most horrific way. Losing her husband to prison. Losing years to her demons before fighting her way through. I can't bear to make things worse, even if none of this is my doing.

A deep breath doesn't do much to ease the guilt. "We think it might be the killer. Maddie's killer."

Her mouth falls open and her eyes go wide before a disbelieving laugh bursts from her. "No. Impossible. Why would he?" she whispers, shaking her head. She even backs away until she bumps into the doorframe.

"To get back at me for hunting him?" I suggest. "I can't say for sure. It's only a theory. When I couldn't get a hold of you … " I whisper, wiping away tears that won't seem to stop falling. "I thought the worst. I'm sorry. I was beside myself."

"I always leave my phone here when I go for a jog," she explains in a soft, sort of vague voice. "It's too distracting, having it with me."

"Maybe it would be a better idea to take it with you from now on," Mitch gently suggests. "What if you had fallen on a patch of ice and couldn't call for help?"

Her brows draw together before she dips her chin, scowling at the suggestion. "I'll have you know I've been running on these streets since way back before the time of cell phones," she retorts. "In all kinds of weather."

It seems almost perverse, the fact that I would laugh at a time like this. There's something about the way she says it and the way she scowls at him like she's insulted that sends a giggle bubbling up into my throat.

But there is nothing funny about this situation. And for all I know, just because Mom is safe and sound now doesn't mean Madeline's killer doesn't have plans for her.

"I think we need to sit down, all of us," I decide. "Mom, there're a few more things I need to fill you in on. Maybe you'll understand better once I do."

Although I'm not sure she will. I already know the facts and still can't understand why any of this is happening.

7

ALEXIS

"Can I get anyone some fresh coffee?" Mom walks around with a pot in hand, filling the cups of anyone who holds theirs out for more. "I have muffins warming in the oven. I'll bring them out for you now."

"Mom, you don't have to go to all this trouble." I may as well be talking to myself as she hurries from the room where we've been sitting with Andy Cobb and a couple deputies for the past half hour. It was Mitch who suggested I call over to let Captain Felch know Mom was alive and well. Otherwise, I may have completely forgotten. The captain insisted on sending Andy out and promised to join us after finishing up a handful of reports related to the Alyssa Lawrence case which we've barely finished closing.

Andy frowns down at the notes he's taken before picking up the note from the coffee table, still encased in its baggie. "So it was this and the slashed tires. Any other evidence around the truck? Footprints, maybe?"

"I wasn't exactly waiting around to identify those," I retort before I can remind myself we're on the same team. Andy and I have butted heads on more than one occasion in the past, mostly resulting from his resentment of my presence. Local detectives don't much enjoy the implications of an FBI agent being brought in to assist on a case. Part of me thinks he's waiting anxiously for me to be reassigned, and is more than likely disappointed that time has yet to come.

There's none of that in his demeanor now, I'm glad to find. "You said this isn't the first note you've gotten from this guy."

"Not exactly something I wanted to broadcast around the station," I offer, but for some reason, I still feel slightly guilty. It's not his business, yet he looks and sounds like he feels personally insulted. "But yes, this is the second note he's left—assuming it's the same person."

"Has that letter been processed?"

Now, I remember the call I received before the discovery this morning. Tyler Mahoney. The name rings out in my head like a bell. "The lab in Virginia got a partial print and made an ID."

Mom is re-entering the room when the doorbell chimes, so she changes her route and heads that way with a plate of muffins in one hand. "Mrs. Forrest? I'm Captain Felch."

"Captain, of course, everyone's in the parlor. Can I get you a cup of coffee?" This is an entirely bizarre situation, yet Mom is every inch the gracious hostess as she leads Captain Felch into the front room.

"Thank you." He takes the muffins from her and places them on the coffee table, where the officers descend on them.

"You should eat," Mitch murmurs. I know he's right, but I can't bring myself to care much about my appetite when there's a man out there determined to destroy me. At least, that's how it feels right now. I'm sure once the shock of the situation wears off, I'll be able to see all of this through clearer eyes. That time hasn't come yet.

Rather than pick up a muffin, I fill Captain Felch in on the phone call I received from the lab this morning. "Apparently, this guy was working at a country club on Martha's Vineyard back in the nineties. A lifeguard."

"Ironic," he muses as he removes his hat, placing it on his lap once he's taken a seat in an armchair across from the sofa. "Saving lives in what might have turned out to be his hunting ground." The grim description makes me shiver. How many girls like my sister swam at that club?

"We'll have to look into any unsolved cases on Martha's Vineyard related to the country club's members," I muse. "We'll need to have the lab process this latest note for prints, as well. He was pretty careful with the other one, though. All they got was a partial."

"The fact is," Felch says, "as much as I hesitate to jump to conclusions, the same familiar tone exists in both messages. It only makes sense that the same person wrote both. Otherwise, you have two stalkers, and I can't imagine why."

Mitch closes a hand over my knee like the idea worries him. I wish I had it in me to offer a little comfort, but I am still reeling from what I can only think of as a close call. I can't even bring myself to tell Mom to calm down and stop fussing so much, since I understand too well the anxiety she's trying to process and move on from. It's not every day a person finds out someone left a threatening note about them, implying they would attack.

"I get the feeling this is the same person," I murmur. "I feel it."

Forest of Lies

"The guy is completely out of his mind." Mitch squeezes my knee hard enough to make me shoot him a surprised look. His jaw is tightly clenched, color rising in his cheeks. "This is kind of a game to him. Seeing how far he can go, sitting back and laughing at the way he can get everyone worked up. It's not enough that he takes lives. He has to ruin everyone around them, too."

I don't know why I never imagined Mitch giving much thought to any of this. I suppose it's easier for me to imagine him brushing it off the way I tried to. How naïve can I be?

"No doubt he's got a few screws loose," the captain agrees while the rest of the men grunt. "But I'm not sure. I think it might go deeper than that."

The room goes silent. I'm sure I could hear a pin drop. Mom re-enters, carrying a mug of steaming coffee, and her gaze bounces around when she finds us staring at each other. "What did I miss?" she asks, sounding like she's not sure she wants the answer.

The captain clears his throat and offers a smile as he accepts the coffee. "Thank you so much. I was about to share a theory I've been mulling over the past few weeks."

"You haven't shared any theories with me," I point out.

"Yes, and with good reason. I didn't want to worry you if you hadn't already considered it yourself. Since you never mentioned it, I imagined you hadn't." He takes a sip of the fragrant brew and his brows lift. "This is delicious."

"I'm going to crawl out of my skin in another second if you don't explain yourself." I'm trying to sound lighthearted, but I'm not very successful. The fact is, the way he's staring at me has an unnerving quality to it.

"It could be he's developed an obsession with you. I'm sorry," he quickly adds when Mom gasps. "I don't want to upset anyone, but that's where the facts lead me. He's going out of his way to alert Alexis to his presence in her life. He's tracked her to the station, where she found the first note. He's tracked her to Mitch's house, where she found the second. He's familiar enough with Mitch to recognize his truck. He has made it his business to learn all he can about you," he concludes, lifting a shoulder and wincing like he's sorry. "It's ugly, but it's more obvious all the time."

"Why Alexis?" Mom sandwiches me between her and Mitch, wedging herself by my side and wrapping an arm around mine.

"Who's to say? She's come closer to tracking him down than anyone has over all these years. It could be he sees something special in her and feels threatened, so he wants to turn the tables and unnerve her to the point where she is unable to investigate for fear of retribution. Or … " He trails off, looking regretful.

"Or?" Mitch prompts.

"Or, he could feel a connection through Madeline."

And here I was, thinking I was the profiler. He's managed to sum the whole thing up succinctly. His theories are sound. I can't think of a way to disprove them, no matter how much I want to.

"How am I supposed to let you out of my sight after today?" Mitch murmurs, and I lean against him, releasing a soft sigh. Between him and Mom, I doubt I'll have a moment to myself until Tyler Mahoney is behind bars where he belongs.

"We can keep a detail on the house," Andy suggests, looking to Captain Felch for confirmation. "It might not be a bad idea to have eyes on your store, too, Mr. Dutton."

I can tell from Mitch's sharp intake of breath that he'll have a strong opinion about this. His opinion is forgotten, though, when a call comes in over the radios the deputies wear. "All units, we have reports of a fire at the Camptown Trailer Park. Fire and medical on the way to the scene. 34 Massachusetts Lane."

34 Massachusetts Lane. My heart stops and my breath comes short because I know that address.

I look at Mom. I see the fear in her eyes, fear that must be reflected in mine. She knows the address, too. She might not go out there to visit, but she wouldn't be able to resist keeping an eye on the man she loved and looked after for so many years.

"Dad," I whisper.

8

ALEXIS

It's barely nine o'clock in the morning, yet for the second time today I'm racing to a parent's home and silently praying they're okay. Again, Mitch is driving, only this time we ride in grim, breathless silence while following behind the captain's car. He has his dome light flashing, parting traffic so we can get there faster.

"Arson is not his MO, is it?" It's the first thing Mitch has said since we practically fled Mom's house after the call came through. Rather, I fled. He followed, shouting at me not to think about driving.

"Who knows anymore?" I mutter in despair. "He wants to keep us guessing." I don't have it in me to hypothesize anymore. Not now, when my father's home is on fire. Is he there? Did he make it out? He had to. There is no other way this can turn out. Life has a way of being terribly unfair, but hasn't he been through his share of tragedy? When is it going to be enough?

A thin line of smoke pierces the gray, cloudy morning sky as we come closer to the trailer park. Before long, the acrid odor overwhelms my senses even with the windows rolled up. There are flashing lights up ahead and plenty of bystanders by the time we reach the perimeter of the cordoned-off area surrounding Dad's trailer.

At first, my brain doesn't want to believe what's in front of me. It refuses. There is no way this is real, that any of this is actually happening. There is no way the entire trailer has been reduced to nothing more than a smoking hulk.

"Wait!" Mitch calls out, but it's too late for that. I'm already halfway out of the truck by the time he's put it in park, pushing my way through the crowd without bothering to excuse myself. I barely hear the cries of surprise and alarm that ring out around me.

"Stay back!" Captain Felch catches me by the arm as I'm about to duck under the caution tape that's been stretched from the mailbox in front of the trailer to the mailbox of the trailer beside it.

One of the firefighters notices us and approaches, scowling. "What do you think you're doing? We're still working the scene. It isn't safe."

Mitch reaches me and pulls me against him. "This is her father's trailer," he explains while looping an arm around my shoulders and holding me in place.

"Sorry to hear that," the man replies, glancing at me. "But we can't let anybody past the tape."

"What happened?" Captain Felch asks. "What do we know?"

The man's tiny smirk is enough to bring my blood to a simmer. "This isn't the time to discuss things in front of civilians, Captain."

"She's an FBI agent," Mitch tells him in a voice that's dangerously close to a growl. "And I'm not going anywhere, with all due respect. What do you know so far? What happened?"

The firefighter's stern expression softens a little. "That's what we're going to have to find out. It didn't take much to extinguish the blaze, but until our investigators comb through, there's no way of knowing how it started."

"His car isn't here," I realize, gripping Mitch's hand like it's the only thing still tethering me to reality. Maybe it is. How much can a person go through in the span of only a few hours? I've already feared for Mom's life, I've dealt with the knowledge that Tyler Mahoney is stalking not just me but the people I love. Now this.

Is it all connected? That's what I don't know. What I need to know. Did Tyler do this?

"It could be he wasn't here when it happened," Mitch muses, rubbing my shoulder while the firefighter goes back to his job and the captain wanders off to ask questions of the officers who were here when we arrived. Several of the other firefighters are milling around, one of them spraying water on a spot that keeps smoking.

The entire scene is too grim and sad for me to process. It wasn't much, but this was all he had. As much as I would hate to think of him coming home and finding it all gone, that would still be better than the alternative.

What if he were inside? What if he were sleeping at the time the fire broke out? It isn't smoke that brings tears to my eyes. He's been through so much. What if this is all it takes to set him back with his sobriety?

I'll be there for him. I'll move in with him someplace else if I have to, so long as he has the support he needs. I'll do anything if it means helping him.

"I can't believe this is happening," I whisper, and Mitch holds me a little tighter.

"I know," he whispers in my ear. "It's all unbelievable. But we can't lose hope. The car's gone, meaning he might've been gone. It could've been faulty wiring that did it. Happens all the time."

Forest of Lies

One of the women standing nearby approaches, looking concerned and maybe a little regretful. The way a person does when they know they're intruding and wish they weren't. "Excuse me. Did I hear someone say you're Mr. Forrest's daughter?" she asks with pity in her eyes and voice.

"I am," I murmur, turning to her. There is plain emotion etched across her weathered, worried face, and her hand trembles as she uses it to hold the collar of her coat closed against the chill in the air.

"Oh, this is so terrible," she mourns, clicking her tongue. "He's such a wonderful man. Everyone around here thinks so. The kindest neighbor. So helpful. He'd give you the shirt off his back in subzero temperatures, that man."

"That's very kind of you to say… " I trail off, raising my brows.

"Oh, I'm Loretta," she explains. "I live two doors down. Your dad shovels my pathway before I even get the chance to ask for help. I'll wake up in the morning, and it's already done."

My chest aches and my throat tightens as affection and dread fight for control. "That sounds like something he'd do," I whisper, trying to smile for her sake.

"He always talked about his daughter who's in the FBI," she continues. "Is that you?"

The lump in my throat won't allow me to answer, so I settle for nodding. "He's so proud of you," she murmurs, patting my arm. "Always talking about how brilliant you are and how good you are at your job."

She's doing her best to comfort me, but her words are like a red hot poker driven into my chest, digging around, burning my heart the way dad's trailer burned. I can't think of anything to say. Somehow I feel like she needs to be comforted, too, which is silly. I'm the one whose father might be in that burned out wreck only yards from where we're standing.

"Out of curiosity," Mitch murmurs, "did you see or hear anything strange this morning?"

She grimaces, her teeth sinking into her lip as she casts a distraught look toward what's left of the trailer. "I can't say I did, but then I'm a very heavy sleeper. It's usually pretty quiet around here, too, at least in the morning. Evenings might be different, but I suppose that's true anywhere."

"I can't believe this," I whisper, shaking. Mitch draws me closer and I turn away from Loretta, pressing my face against his coat. I hear her murmuring her apologies, and I hear Mitch murmuring in reply, but nothing makes any sense. They may as well be talking gibberish. I can hardly hear them over the pounding of my heart. He was trying so hard to pull his life together. He has already suffered so much. It's too unfair. I can't lose him.

"He may have gone away for a couple of days," Mitch reasons, quietly murmuring in my ear while he almost rocks me from side to side like he's comforting a baby. "We don't know yet. Have you tried to call him?"

No, it hadn't even occurred to me for some reason. I fumble with my phone and pull up his number, closing my eyes as I raise it to my ear. One ring. Two rings. It's like the situation with Mom all over again, praying he'll answer like I prayed she would.

And much like that situation, all I get is Dad's voicemail greeting. It's not like him to ignore my calls, and he's never been a late sleeper. Then again, if he is away on a little vacation, his schedule might've changed. There's nothing saying he had to inform me of his plans. We don't touch base on a daily basis, something I regret more than I can handle now as I stand here, waiting to find out whether he burned up in his bed.

When a pair of firefighters go inside, I almost can't bear to watch. "Please, please," I whisper, then hold my breath with all of my focus tuned to the wreckage. The quiet chatter that's filled the smoky morning air until this point cuts off all at once. It's like somebody flipped a switch or turned the volume knob all the way down.

Captain Felch rejoins us, looking grim. He doesn't say a word and doesn't need to. Everything he's thinking is plain on his sad, worried face. He doesn't have it in him to offer empty assurances. I'm glad, since I don't have it in me to accept them.

When one of the firemen emerges and shakes his head, I sag in Mitch's arms. I know what that means – if there were a body inside, he would motion for a stretcher and a body bag. The second man follows him, and I hear his simple two-word announcement even over the deafening rush of blood in my ears. "All clear."

"He wasn't home," Mitch tells me, holding me up, clutching me tight while everyone around us reacts with relief. "He wasn't here. It's okay."

And he's right – at least, partly. Because I barely have a chance to breathe easily before an entirely new set of circumstances bubble to the surface. He may not have been there, but where is he? I won't have a peaceful moment until I get a hold of him.

First, I call Mom, fighting back tears of relief and gratitude. "The trailer's wrecked, but he wasn't inside," I manage before the dam breaks and I'm left leaning against Mitch for support all over again. "He wasn't inside, and his car is missing. He might not have been anywhere around when it happened."

"Oh, thank goodness," she whimpers before bursting into tears. For a little while, that's all either of us can do, crying together while what's left of my father's humble home sits smoking in front of me.

9

ALEXIS

"Are you sure you want to go in?" Mitch makes it a point to speak quietly as he hands me a pair of lattes which I wedge carefully into a cardboard carrier with the intention of taking it to the station. It's almost a joke at this point, bringing coffee to the captain every morning. The more he insists I don't need to do it, the more determined I am to bring it with me. He should know better by now. I am very stubborn when I decide to be.

"I have to." And it's the truth. I might feel like my brain is made of chewing gum after barely getting a minute of sleep last night, but I can't bear the idea of sitting all day with nothing to do but worry.

As it is, I did more than enough of that yesterday. Mom was in a pretty fragile state, putting it mildly. It doesn't take much imagination to understand why.

She's gone from finding out a killer threatened her life to worrying about the life of her ex-husband. Yes, he avoided burning up in the trailer, but there is still the question of where he is now. And why he's gone all this time without returning my many, many calls and texts.

Mitch glances over my shoulder at the line of people forming behind me, then waves one of his employees over to handle them while he steps aside with me. "You can't keep pushing yourself like this. Pretty soon, it's going to be too much."

I close my eyes and force myself to focus solely on the touch of his hand against my cheek. As always, he's tender, patient, and it would be easy to dismiss his tenderness in the face of my anxiety. That certainly wouldn't do me any favors, and it wouldn't do much for our relationship, either. He's been nothing but strong and supportive through all of this, even bringing dinner over to the house last night so we wouldn't have to worry about cooking.

"I'm not going because I'm addicted to work," I whisper, covering his hand with mine and wrapping my fingers around his. "I'm going because I'll lose it if I don't. I need something to do. I have to distract myself somehow."

"I'm sure there are people out there looking for him. They're giving it their all."

I love him for trying so hard to reassure me, but there's a hole in his logic. If they're working so hard to find him, why haven't they done it yet? Where can he be?

"Then let's just say I want to be right there whenever a call comes in," I suggest. "I don't want to have to wait for somebody to fill me in, you know? It'll be fine. I'm behind on reports, anyway."

He doesn't look convinced, sighing softly before shrugging. "All right. I know better than to try to get through to you when you're dead set on a course of action." He brushes his lips against my forehead before sighing again. "Do me a favor and keep me posted at all times. No running off to chase down a lead without checking in. Can you do that for me?"

"Sure, I will." After everything that went down yesterday, not to mention the drama we only recently worked our way through, communication is more important than ever. I need him too badly to risk ruining us.

I notice a couple of curious looks from other patrons as I make my way out of the store. No doubt they recognize me and heard about the fire. Dad makes it a point to avoid people in town after the scandal following the shooting and his imprisonment, but they remember him. No one says anything to me, but they don't need to. I hear the questions in their heads, and it's a relief to escape them and step outside into a bitterly cold but brilliantly sunny morning.

Though there was not a single sound from my phone the entire time I was inside, I have to check it as soon as I'm behind the wheel and warming up the car. My frustration gets a little worse every time I check with nothing to show for it. Why won't he call me back? Where could he be? If he knew he would be out of touch for even a day, he would've told me so.

Wouldn't he? Maybe he forgot, which I can't pretend makes me feel much better. Nobody wants to be reminded their relationship with a parent isn't as close as they would like it to be. I should be there for him more. I should make myself a bigger part of his life. There are so many things I'll do differently from now on if I get the chance. I only need the chance.

I'm barely inside the station, cup carrier in hand, when Captain Felch appears seemingly out of nowhere and pulls me aside, into an empty interrogation room. "What are you doing here?"

"Bringing your coffee, obviously." I don't know where I get this perverse need to tease him a little when I know very well what he means. It must be a defense mechanism of some sort. My way of proving I'm all right, that this isn't going to break me.

He's not impressed, only scowling more deeply. "You know what I mean. This is the last place you need to be, and I didn't expect you to come in. Besides," he reminds me in an almost regretful voice, "you don't work here. No one expects you to clock in or out."

"I don't work here? Then why do I have reports that need to be finished?"

He clicks his tongue with a sigh. "You know very well what I meant."

"I do, and do you know what I mean when I tell you I need to be here. I can't wait around, sitting on my hands."

"All right," he relents, taking one of the cups from the carrier.

"What have I missed?" I ask as we leave the room and continue toward his office.

"Not much. There hasn't been a hit on the all-points bulletin on your father's car. State police are out there looking for him. We're going to find him."

"What if we can't?"

He sighs heavily, stopping at his office door. "What if the world stops turning tomorrow?"

"That's not very nice. I'm serious."

"So am I, and I don't mean to sound flippant," he assures me. "But the point remains. Asking *'what if'*

Forest of Lies

never gets us anywhere. All we can do is move forward, take things one step at a time, and do our best. Right?"

"Right." I'm glad his office phone rings when it does. It gives me an excuse to continue down the hall while he answers the call, so I can retreat to the solitude of my makeshift office. I was never supposed to be around here as long as I've been. This was never going to be permanent. Yet here I remain, taking off my coat and hanging it over the back of the chair, placing my laptop on the desk and opening it up.

The last thing I feel like doing today is working on reports. That's never been exactly my favorite thing to do in the first place. I can't think of anyone who would rather sit at their desk and type out their notes than engage in actual work.

It might be the best thing for me now. It forces me to focus, since I would like to be finished with this as quickly as possible. Going over the circumstances of the Alyssa Lawrence case leaves me wondering how her kids are doing. Has Connor explained to them why their mother has been away? Probably not – they're too young to understand. But they must wonder. Kids at that age tend to ask incessant questions until they receive an explanation that suits them. My heart goes out to him even now, as I fear for my father's life.

What if. Those two words echo in my skull, bringing with them incessant questions. What if the note on Mitch's truck was only a diversion? What if Tyler led me to Mom before going to the trailer park and attacking his real victim? I wouldn't put it past him to use me to lure Dad away somehow. The more I think about it, the more convinced I am that it's exactly the sort of thing he would do. Just like he used Mom against me.

Still, Dad's car hasn't been spotted yet, and there are state troopers looking high and low for it. If someone did hurt Dad, they would have had to dispose of the car somehow.

Stop. Later. I need to compartmentalize, and fast. The longer I sit here going through the possibilities, the more panicked and disjointed I feel. Work is the only tool I've ever used to cope with stress. It's my only means of distracting myself, of keeping myself from tumbling over the edge into an abyss of blind, screaming fear. If I can't focus on it, I'm lost. There's no hope for me. And I won't be any help to either of my parents should they need me.

I won't be any help to myself, either. Right now, though, that seems pretty unimportant. Mitch might disagree, but I would expect nothing less.

I shake out my hands and pull the chair a little closer to the desk, determined to dive back into my work.

Forest of Lies

Unfortunately, I'm interrupted before I can type a single word. The captain doesn't usually barge in without at least knocking or clearing his throat to alert me to his presence. The fact that he comes straight in without hesitating sends my heart leaping into my throat. "What happened? What have you heard?" I croak.

His mouth moves, but at first, nothing comes out. His eyes dart around the room, and his throat works before he manages to offer an explanation. "It's not your father," he mumbles, running a hand over his head and down the back of his neck. "I might need to ask a favor of you, though."

Considering everything he's done for me, I owe him a hundred favors – at least. Then there's the selfish part of me that longs for a distraction. "Anything. Whatever you need."

He takes a shuddering breath before releasing it slowly. "The call that just came in. It was to let me know someone in my family has gone missing."

10

ALEXIS

I've never seen the captain like this, but then nothing we've ever worked on has involved someone he cares about. I can't help but think back on just a few minutes ago, when he was the one trying to calm me down before I could spiral out of control. I should know by now how quickly life can turn. One minute, everything is going smoothly, status quo. The next, all you can do is wish things would go back to the way they used to be. Life can be cruel that way.

I won't bother telling him to calm down, and I won't feed him any half-baked assurances. For one thing, I don't know this person, so I can't in good faith insist he would never do anything like this. All I can do is wait until Captain Felch comes to a stop after pacing aimlessly for a while, then ask, "Who did the call come from?"

"My sister, Becky." His heavy brows draw together like he's pained. "She's a wreck. Beside herself. This is the first time anything like this has ever happened."

"How old are they?"

"Pete is fourteen." Before I have time to process this, he shoots me a warning look. "Don't go there."

"Go where?" I ask, a little surprised.

"This isn't some typical fourteen-year-old who decides he doesn't like following the rules and wants to prove he's capable of being on his own without anyone telling him what to do." He shakes his head firmly, even folding his arms like he expects an argument. "That's not him. He's not that kind of kid, and he never has been. I know it's easy for me to say as his uncle, but I've known him since he was born." His voice cracks slightly, and it isn't lost on me that this is the first time he's ever had a reason to show emotion like this. "He wouldn't run away."

She wouldn't run away. Of all times for me to have a flashback. I can still see my parents sitting together in the front parlor, holding hands and sitting close together while being questioned in the hours following my sister's disappearance. *She would never have done something like this.*

I knew it, too. I was as sure of my sister's habits and activities as I was of my own. I knew, like they did, there was no way she ever would have picked up and walked off. Not Maddie.

"It could be a case of a fourteen-year-old being a fourteen-year-old," I offer. I have to tread lightly, choose my words carefully, especially since his sister isn't the only one beside herself. "Maybe he spent the night at a friend's house and didn't check in?"

"It's not like that." Finally, he takes a seat, almost collapsing into a chair in front of my desk. "He's the most conscientious kid you've ever met. Good grades, never misses curfew, even helps take care of the house as much as he can while Becky is working. I can't tell you how many times she's said she could never make it through without him. I know it sounds like an uncle refusing to see the writing on the wall," he insists. "I have kids of my own. I know what to look for. He's not some careless teenager."

In a gentler voice, I ask, "Exactly what happened?"

"Becky's been working herself to death," he tells me with a sigh. "In some ways, you remind me of her. Only in her case, a lot of it has to do with covering legal bills. She and her husband, Andrew, are in the middle of divorce proceedings."

And their teenaged son has gone missing. I am not one to let my prejudices get in the way of a case, but it sort of seems the writing is on the wall. Maybe it takes someone standing on the outside to see clearly.

Forest of Lies

"She got home from work this morning and assumed he was at school since his bedroom was empty and she hadn't gotten word of him being absent," he continues, sitting back and rubbing his temples. "Normally, by the time she wakes up in the afternoon, he's home. That was when she knew something had to be wrong, when she called the school and they told her he never showed up today."

The poor woman probably thought she was still asleep, dreaming—or else she wished she was. "What about the father? Could Pete have spent the night there?"

"Becky says no. Pete wouldn't voluntarily spend the night with his father." He rolls his eyes before his lips settle into a firm, disapproving line. "He's living with some bartender who worked for him. Hence the divorce proceedings."

"Oh. I see." So far, all I'm getting is the profile of a potentially troubled boy. His parents split up, Dad's living with a girlfriend, Mom's struggling to get by and Pete's trying to pick up the slack wherever he can. From where I'm sitting, it's pretty much textbook.

"He's a quiet kid," the captain insists. "He's got a bedroom full of science-fiction and fantasy books. He doesn't have a lot of friends, but he's not the loner type, either. He would rather read or play video games than play sports. And he would never,

ever do something like this to Becky. That much, I'm sure of."

"And he's never done anything like this before? That you know of, I mean?

"No," he insists before blurting out a silent, humorless laugh. "Do you know how difficult it is to assure someone there's a logical explanation for something, when you've seen for yourself countless times how life can be?"

"I do," I remind him gently. "I can't tell you how many times I've had to politely push aside everything I know, and all of the experiences I've had, to comfort a family member. It isn't easy."

"No," he agrees, looking sick. "No. It's not easy at all."

There is an obvious question hanging in the air between us, and I don't know of any polite way to voice it. The last thing I want is to come off uncaring, especially when he has never been anything but supportive and concerned. Clearing my throat, I shift uncomfortably in my seat before I have to ask, "What is it you need from me? What can I do?"

"I need your help," he blurts out, point blank. "I can't personally involve myself with this. I'm connected to … the subject." He swallows hard and my heart goes out to him. He looks a lot like a man who wishes he could wake up from his nightmare, and I can only relate.

"I don't know that this is quite a case for the FBI," I point out as carefully as I can.

"It's not the FBI aspect I'm interested in. You have those instincts of yours." With his elbows on his knees, he leans forward, and there's a hint of desperation in his gaze. He's liable to burn a hole in me, staring at me the way he is. "You've always been able to see through half-baked stories and excuses. Please, if you could ask questions and do a little digging, it would mean the world to Becky, I'm sure. And to me," he adds as an afterthought. "I have to help her somehow. This is the only means I can imagine."

"I understand."

He lowers his head, lacing his fingers behind the back of his neck. "He's all she has now," he murmurs to the floor. I have to look away – it seems wrong, witnessing his despair. Like I'm peeking in on something I wasn't supposed to see. "She's always been so proud of him. The one thing she never had to worry about. That's how she always described him. Conscientious to a fault. Always exactly where he says he'll be. He was born old—that's something we've always said."

That sounds familiar, too, only this time I'm reminded of the way grownups described me when I was a kid. Older than my years, that sort of thing.

I don't have the heart to tell the captain now that sometimes, it's the kids everyone depends on who are more likely to wish they could break free. I could never have done that to Mom and Dad, not after Maddie … but there were times the idea was appealing. Shrugging off the sense of responsibility I always bore, wishing I could be somebody else. If that's what Pete had in mind, I certainly hope he was at least smart about it. That he didn't somehow fall in with the wrong people. A mother who works crazy shifts and isn't home to see her son off to school? I'm sure Becky does her absolute best, but she can't be with him all the time.

One thing is for sure. "I'll help you in any way I can," I promise. "Whatever I can do. You just tell me what you need."

"You don't know what a relief it is to hear that." He releases a shuddering sigh. "To start, I called Andrew and asked him to come in. He'll bring the girl with him. Brittany, if I remember correctly. Becky was sure Pete wouldn't have spent the night there, at least not without telling her so, but we have to start somewhere."

"When are they expected?"

Forest of Lies

He checks his watch. "Fifteen minutes or so?"

I was looking for a way to distract myself from my worries over Dad, wasn't I? Sometimes, the universe responds in the most unusual way.

11

ALEXIS

I have around fifteen minutes to pull myself together and get a few things in order. I was planning on heading back to Mom's as soon as my reports were finished. I don't like leaving her alone at a time like this, with Dad missing and no idea of where he could be. They've been divorced almost as long as they were married, but I doubt that's enough to eliminate the feelings that once kept them together. It isn't that their divorce was particularly ugly – if anything, I've always theorized he pushed for it, determined to set her free. I was too young at the time for anyone to discuss the finer points with me, but the years have granted me a little insight.

As always, I turn to the one person who never lets me down. When Mitch answers the call, there's clear concern in his greeting. "What is it? Any news?"

Forest of Lies

I can't help but warm inside when I hear him. "Nothing about Dad at the moment," I tell him with a defeated sigh. "I keep getting his voicemail. How's it going with you?"

"I got the truck back," he announces. "Brand-new tires. I needed them soon, anyway."

I'm glad to hear his positive spin on things, even if it boils my blood beyond belief that they were ever slashed. "It's good you're feeling upbeat, since I'm about to ask for a huge favor."

"What's up? Are you all right?"

"Define all right," I counter with a dry chuckle. "I need your help. There's a missing kid the captain needs my help with. It's his nephew," I murmur, observing the captain through the windows lining one wall of my office. I've never seen him look so aimless as he almost wanders around, raking his fingers through his hair, even muttering to himself. "He can't be personally involved in the investigation, and he asked me to question the kid's father."

Mitch clicks his tongue. "That's a shame. He thinks the father might have something to do with it?"

"There's no way of knowing. Right now, it's a matter of finding out what we can. Which means I can't get out of here just yet. I was hoping to go and spend some time with Mom. She's been beside herself." Not that I need to tell him that. He's been by my side all the way and has witnessed Mom's ups and downs as she cycles from fear to dread to assuring us everything will be fine and back again.

"She has a reason to be." He doesn't keep me waiting, only pausing for a moment before adding, "Of course, I'll go over and check in with her. She shouldn't be alone – then again, neither should you."

I have to laugh as I gaze out over the station from my back office. "I'm hardly alone."

"You know what I mean. There's a difference between being in a station full of people and feeling like you're supported."

It's important at times like this to notice and appreciate the little moments of light. Bright spots in the darkness. Otherwise, it would be too easy to sink into oblivion and let the darkness swallow me.

I lean back in my chair, grinning and closing my eyes as I imagine Mitch in front of me. "It's a good thing I have you in my life, because you always make me feel supported. No matter whether we're together or miles apart."

"You know, if you ever decide to give up on law enforcement, you could make a career as a greeting card writer."

He always knows how to make me laugh, even in the most difficult circumstances. Yet another reason why

I couldn't get by without him. "I'm keeping my options open."

He growls softly, which only makes my grin widen. "So long as you don't keep them open with me. I'm sort of learning to like keeping an eye on you."

"Don't worry. I'm not letting you go anywhere." It's so nice, being able to retreat to us for a little while. It's enough to joke together, to take a few breaths, and remember that not everything in the world is grim and fraught with questions. "Oh, and don't be surprised if you see a patrol car hanging around. I don't want to take any chances."

"I'm sure it will make your mom feel better to know there are eyes on the house." He chuckles softly before adding, "I'm sure it makes you feel better, too."

"Just a little." But not entirely. I'm never going to stop worrying, ever. It's an impossibility. So long as I know Tyler is out there—having a name to attach to him makes him that much more real—I won't be able to truly rest. Especially now that I know he likes to play games.

I promise to give Mitch a call once I'm finished questioning Andrew McClintock, then end the call and head to the ladies room to freshen up a little. I wasn't planning on conducting interviews today, and I need to get into the correct headspace. A few splashes of cold water against my cheeks makes them tingle, and I actually look somewhat alive when I meet my gaze in the mirror. I have to compartmentalize. It won't do Pete any favors if I'm distracted and groggy.

Would Tyler do something like this? It fits his profile, top to bottom. The right age, for sure, and while most of his victims were female there were a couple of boys in the mix.

I would think he's been too busy messing with me to turn his attention elsewhere. *Rule number one: do not assume.* There is no using reason to make sense of any of this. I can't think the way I do. I need to think the way he does, as twisted and dark an idea as that is.

For all I know, Tyler could have kidnapped Pete to up the chaos factor and split my attention. I can't find him if I'm busy trying to find the child he abducted.

What if this isn't about me at all? I would rather it wasn't, of course. Who wouldn't? And I would hate to imagine this child and his mother suffering all because Tyler Mahoney wants to prove a point, that he has the power to destroy lives at will.

All of the self-questioning in the world isn't going to get me anywhere. I splash my face again before waving my hand beneath the motion sensor controlled towel dispenser. A few deep breaths as I blot my face dry help slow my heart rate, but only a little. What if Tyler is behind this? What if he did something to Dad?

What am I talking about? He already has. Tyler destroyed my father's life when he lured Maddie away from the family who adored her.

I step out of the ladies room to find Captain Felch leading a couple back to one of the interrogation rooms. I have the opportunity to observe them for a moment before I'm noticed. At first, it's surprising to find Andrew McClintock walking beside a girl I might mistake for his daughter if it weren't for the protective arm he's draped around her waist. There is something decidedly non-parental about it.

Could that be the girl he had the affair with? She might have turned twenty-one last week by the looks of it, though I'm tired and my eyesight might be suffering for it. I notice the way she rubs her belly, which also takes me by surprise. The captain didn't mention the happy couple is expecting a baby. She's decently far along from the looks of it, maybe five or six months, and she can't seem to keep her hand off her bump as Captain Felch has a quiet discussion with Andrew.

I have to admit, he at least looks the part of a worried parent. I'm sure he cares about his son, even if his marriage was not at the top of his priority list.

He's grim, even stricken, firing questions at the captain before the three of them disappear into one of the rooms.

While I know I should head straight inside after them, I have to check one more time. A quick call to Dad's phone gets me no closer to speaking with him, unfortunately. I shoot Mitch a quick text on my way down the hall. **Could you please give Dad a call for me? I'm on my way in to interview the family, so I won't be able to do it myself.**

I have to wonder what good it will do as I add Dad's number to the message. The point is to feel like I'm covering my bases. Like I'm doing more than sitting on my hands and waiting. Worrying. Dreading.

I'm not doing Pete any favors by splitting my attention, and I wouldn't want to speak to an agent who was too distracted by personal problems to be of any help. It's with that in mind that I throw my shoulders back and remind myself I'm a professional.

Even if all I want more than anything in the world is a hug from my daddy.

12

ALEXIS

The phone in my pocket feels a lot heavier than it should I step into the room, where Felch is still engaged in a conversation with his brother-in-law. He waves me in while explaining, "Andrew, Brittany, this is Agent Alexis Forrest. She was sent up from Boston on another case and has been working with us ever since."

"The FBI?" Andrew McClintock is a man in his mid-forties by the looks of it. A good looking man for his or any other age, with only the faintest hint of silver strands threading through his otherwise thick, black hair. The fact that the strands are so sporadically spaced and tend to pick up the light when he moves only adds to his appeal. I can imagine women sitting at his bar, their attention drawn by his icy blue eyes and rugged good looks. I guess he spends a lot of time on the go, always moving, and that shows in his healthy physique.

Those icy eyes of his are decidedly red rimmed as he turns toward the captain in confusion. "You called in the FBI?" he asks as Brittany whimpers softly beside him.

"I haven't been assigned to this case by the field office," I explain, though he wasn't speaking to me. "I happened to be here, and Captain Felch asked for my help. At a time like this, we need all hands on deck."

Andrew runs a hand over his head before shrugging helplessly. "I'm sorry. I just don't know what to think. I keep telling myself I'm going to wake up and this will all be a bad dream." Brittany, meanwhile, rubs his shoulder while murmuring soft reassurances. She looks a little green around the gills, though I don't know if that's the result of worry over Pete or her pregnancy.

"Is there anything I can get you?" I ask her after we shake hands. "Some water? Tea?"

"We have to stop wasting time!" Andrew blurts out before she can answer.

"I'm fine," Brittany tells me with a brief smile before she turns her attention back to Andrew. "They're going to do everything they can. You've got to let these people do their jobs."

"That's good advice." I look to Felch, the two of us having a silent conversation before his shoulders sink a little. It's time for him to get out of here and remove himself from the interview. I have no doubt he'll watch from the monitor in his office, but it's not the same as being here.

He clears his throat before heading for the door. "I won't be far away," he vows. "And I'll come back once Alexis has finished asking questions."

"Asking questions." Andrew bangs his fists against the table hard enough to make both Brittany and me flinch in surprise. "What is the good of any of this? You need to be out there looking for him, not asking questions of people who love him. Pete needs you," he adds, and his red rimmed eyes go watery as he tears up.

It's obvious Captain Felch doesn't know what to say – his face falls in a stricken expression of pain. I raise my hand slightly. "Respectfully, this is part of the process," I murmur as gently as possible. This man is already on the edge, and I can understand why. Still, there's part of me that wants to ask Brittany if this is a normal occurrence. Does he often lose his temper and blow up out of nowhere?

"Listen to her." Brittany rubs his back in slow circles with one hand, rubbing her belly with the other. "They know what they're doing here."

"We do," the captain agrees before opening the door and stepping out. "So does Agent Forrest." Once the door clicks, we're officially alone.

"Do you know what this is like?" Andrew's bloodshot eyes could bore holes into me, blazing with a fire I sadly recognize. I wish I didn't, but I've seen it too many times. The desperation, the heartbreak. Not to mention a sense of utter helplessness. I know how that feels all too well.

"Not exactly," I admit as I take a seat. "But I've been involved with countless cases. I was personally involved in one of them. Not my child, but my sister." I detest bringing that up, turning my sister's horrible death into a means of relating to a heartbroken family member. Then again, it might give her tragic, senseless loss a sense of meaning and purpose.

Andrew releases a sigh, and some of his temper seems to lessen. "And how did your parents deal with it?"

"A lot like you are now," I admit. It helps him, though, letting him sit up a little straighter. His son is still missing, but he doesn't have to feel guilty about falling apart.

"Honestly, there isn't that much we can tell you." It makes sense for Brittany to be the more levelheaded of the two, thanks to her level of detachment from the victim. "And I guess Chris told you he's a great kid."

It's rare for me to hear Captain Felch referred to by his first name, much less a shortened version of it. Now is not the time for me to correct this girl and ask her to show a little respect. I probably know him better than she does, and I wouldn't call him Chris.

That's irrelevant. "Captain Felch did tell me what a great kid Pete is," I assure them, keeping my focus on Andrew. "Quiet, good grades, no trouble."

"That's right. Even with all this ... stuff going on between me and his mom." He squirms a little. Not a lot, just enough for me to see through his words and understand his mindset. There's a good chance he feels a little embarrassed, and it's not like someone in the middle of a contentious divorce enjoys discussing the finer points with a stranger, badge or no badge.

Still, the situation might prove pertinent. "I'm sorry to ask such personal questions, but I would like to know more about your relationship." I wave a hand between them. "I understand it's what led to the divorce proceedings between you and Mrs. McClintock. How do you think that affected Pete? Did his attitude or mannerisms change at all?"

That's not such an easy question to ask. It gives me no pleasure to put someone on the spot, especially when something as touchy as infidelity is the reason for it.

If it was difficult for me to ask, it's twice as bad for Andrew. He shakes his head hard, determined to disprove any theory I might have already conceived. "Not even a little. If anything, he's been on his best behavior to make things easier. That's how he is. He's the only one-year-old I ever saw who didn't smash his fists into his birthday cake. Like… like he was afraid to make a mess." His soft laugh is edged in pain.

"How many times have I said we'd be lucky if our little one turns out like him?" Brittany's smile is a little sad. "He's such a great kid."

A nice segue, and an opportunity to change course and maybe catch them off-guard. "How does he feel about the two of you being together?"

Andrew's eyes widen before he recovers his composure. "Let me get one thing straight here and now." Folding his arms on the table, he pins me in place with a steady, unblinking gaze. "No matter what you might have heard before we arrived, the relationship between Pete's mom and myself had been strained for a long time before the split. My relationship with Brittany was a symptom, not the cause of the split."

"It expedited things," Brittany adds, shrugging.

"I understand." Looking from Brittany to Andrew, I add, "But that doesn't answer my original question. How does Pete feel? What sort of impression did he give you? How does he feel about being a big brother?"

Andrew's sigh pairs well with Brittany's averted gaze. She twirls a strand of blond hair while looking down at the table, her lips pressed together in a thin line. "Look, no kid is ever happy when they feel like their mom is being replaced," Andrew murmurs. "He's a little uncomfortable with it. But if you're trying to imply he would act out over Brittany having a baby and me starting a new family, you're wrong. That's not how he operates."

Not a moment later, the sound of raised voices makes the three of us turn our heads toward the door. "Don't do this, Becky!" I recognize Captain Felch's voice raised in a shout like I've only heard from him while we were entering a suspect's home. Its intensity raises the hair on the back of my neck.

That's not enough to stop who I assume is Becky McClintock from throwing the door open and storming into the room, red-faced, tear-stained, marching straight to the table like she intends to pummel her ex. "You! This is all your fault! None of this would be happening if it weren't for you!"

13

ALEXIS

"Mrs. McClintock?" I'm out of my chair in a heartbeat, placing myself between her and the table where Andrew and Brittany sit. They both lean back, away from her, with Andrew almost draping himself over his pregnant girlfriend in a protective gesture.

"This is on you!" Spit flies from Becky's mouth as she angrily jabs a finger at her ex-husband. "This is all your fault! You did this!"

Andrew raises his head after lowering it close to Brittany's, and there's fire in his eyes again. "Now you know very well I would never—"

Becky cuts him off with a harsh, bitter laugh. "Oh, please. What, are you going to tell me you're above being a terrible father? Next thing you know, you'll tell me you were a great husband, too."

This is getting uglier by the second and is in no way helping Pete. "All right," I finally announce, placing my hands gently but firmly against Becky's shoulders and easing her back. "This is getting us nowhere, Mrs. McClintock."

"And who are you?" It's as if she only just noticed me, her teary eyes darting over my face while an accusatory snarl begins to form. "Get out of my way!" All at once she starts swinging her arm, trying to hit her ex-husband even with me standing between them.

"Becky!" I shout, now moving her away from the table. Once we're halfway across the room, I hold her at arm's length and wait until she meets my gaze. The way she looks at me, it seems she hates me about as much as she does her ex. That's fine. Let her direct her frustration at me if it means avoiding a heartbroken mother being charged with assault.

"Keep her away from us!" Brittany's voice is high-pitched, trembling.

"It's you who should have kept away from us!" Becky counters. She shoots a filthy look at Brittany's baby bump and her lip curls in a sneer. "So, you managed to trap him. Congratulations."

"You don't talk to her that way!" Andrew's shout is barely audible over Brittany's almost deafening shriek.

She follows it by crossing her hands over her belly. "How dare you?" she demands. "Storming in here like this, wasting time with your nasty screaming. No big surprise. Everything is always about you."

"How would you know anything about me?" Becky's already flushed face goes a deeper shade of red. "You don't know the first thing about me, you bitch."

"Okay, okay. Enough of this." I have to steer Becky out of the room with one arm locked firmly around her waist. "It's probably better if you wait for me in another room, all right? When I'm finished with them, I'll come and speak to you."

I doubt she hears me over her hurled insults. "If you had been a decent father, this wouldn't have happened," Becky insists over her shoulder while I usher her out.

Andrew scoffs. "You always need to have the last word, Beck. Good to see that hasn't changed. Maybe for once you'll think about our son instead of your hurt feelings."

Forget being gentle with tormented parents for now. "I said that was enough, and I wasn't only speaking to Becky." My sharp rebuke seems to take a little of the wind out of Andrew's sails. I know nothing about the details of their relationship, really, and at the heart of all of this is a shared concern for a missing boy. I feel like I have to say something. I can't let the two of them tear each other to pieces all because they need someone to take their pain out on.

I look out into the hall and flag down the closest deputy, still holding Becky at my side in case she decides to take a leap over the table. "Can you take Mrs. McClintock to a different room? Grab her some water or coffee if she needs it? I'll be in to see you shortly," I assure her with a pat on her shoulder. "We are doing everything we can, I promise."

"I don't trust her." That's the last thing Becky manages to say before she's led away. The sort of comment that has to be taken with a grain of salt, all things considered. She's talking about a woman who, as far as she's concerned, stole her husband. Naturally, she wouldn't want to trust Brittany. I can't say I blame her for that.

"She doesn't know what she's talking about." Andrew is shaking when I turn back to him and his girlfriend, who looks like she may be rubbing her belly for good luck at this point. Much more, and she'll wear straight through her cable knit sweater. "We had nothing to do with this. Why would I hurt my own son? He … "

He swallows hard before continuing. "That's what I regret. That's the only thing I regret in all of this."

"What do you mean?" I take a seat again, my attention trained on him while Brittany continues sniffling.

"Making him feel like he's caught up in the middle of us. Like he has to pick sides." He looks down at his clenched fists, resting on the table. "That, I wish didn't have to happen. He doesn't deserve it."

Brittany's scoff tells me she does not share his opinion. "If he feels like he has to pick sides, it's because she makes him feel that way."

"And you're sure of that? What gives you that impression?" My gaze bounces back and forth between them, waiting for something to back up her assertion.

Brittany stares expectantly at Andrew for a moment, but it's clear he doesn't feel comfortable speaking. After sighing and rolling her eyes, she explains, "You saw the way she was when she came in here. Throwing blame around. Calling us nasty names. That's not the first time she's tried to cause a scene."

"She's not a bad mom." Andrew's swollen eyes meet mine and hold my gaze like he wants to make sure I understand he means it. "She's always been a good mother. As for where Pete could be now, I really don't know. He never reached out to me, he wasn't scheduled for a visit. You don't know how much I

Forest of Lies

wish I could give you something more than that." He lowers his head into his palms, trembling.

After assuring him we'll contact him as soon as we hear anything, I watch the two of them leave with their arms around each other. At least he has someone to lean on, unlike his ex-wife. I hope Brittany is sturdy enough to bear the weight.

By the time I reach the room where Becky waits, she's much calmer, her hands wrapped around a steaming cup of coffee. "I'm sorry," she mumbles while fishing in her pocket for what turns out to be a tissue which she uses to blow her nose. "But when Chris told me they were here together, I lost it."

"It's understandable." I won't insult her by saying I understand, because I don't. I can't relate. But it's not outside the realm of possibility for a person to break down at a time like this.

"Did he say anything? Did Pete reach out to him or anything?" Desperation rings out loud and clear in her voice. I wish I could comfort her.

Instead, I have to choose my words carefully to manage her fears. "He claims he hasn't heard anything from Pete. But he does seem devastated," I add when she rolls her eyes. "He is very upset, and just as anxious for us to get out there and find your son. And we're trying, really."

She leans back in the chair with her arms folded and releases a shaky sigh. She's younger than the captain, quite pretty… but worn out. The sudden disappearance of her son wouldn't create those lines bracketing her mouth or the ones creasing her forehead. They're the result of time and overwork and sleepless nights. "Can I ask you about your relationship with your husband?" I venture.

"He's not my husband anymore." Scoffing, she adds, "Legally, maybe, but not in spirit. He made sure of that." Only a woman who's had the rug pulled out from under her can manage to sound that bitter and defeated.

Which causes me to question the description of their marriage. "I understand things were poor between you two for a while before—"

In a flash, she holds up a hand, her eyes narrowing. "Pardon? What, did he tell you that?"

"Yes, he did. He said things were bad for a while prior to when his … relationship started."

"That's news to me." When all I can do is stare, she explains. "As far as I was concerned, things were fine. I mean, yes, there are points in any relationship where things get a little tired or stale. You're working long hours, you might not see each other as much as you want to. But when we did, everything seemed fine. We spent all the time together we could

… until we didn't anymore. I should've known when he first dyed his hair."

"When he what?"

"Dyed his hair. You didn't notice?" She laughs softly at my surprise. "No, you wouldn't, since you didn't know him before. It's one of those slow working jobs, you know? He wants to keep it subtle. Trust me, he's a lot more gray under all that dye than he wants you to believe."

"What are you trying to say? He's having a midlife crisis?" Her head bobs up and down, at which point I ask, "Do you think that's what set things off with Brittany?"

She takes her time, examining the cup and her chewed fingernails before sighing. "All I know is, he started coloring his hair, started spending all his time at the bar, started sleeping with his bartender." Pain deepens the lines on her face before she adds, "He started spending less time with Pete, too. They used to play video games together. Sometimes, he would take Pete and his best friend to see movies they were interested in, or to the bookstore to pick up their fantasy books. Weeks went by without the two of them spending any time together at all. That was when I first became sure he was seeing somebody. He was a ghost in our home."

A wry grin flashes across her face. "Why is it men think they can get away with things? It was obvious he was pulling away. From me, from Pete, from everything we were building together."

I have no time to process this before there's a knock at the door. It opens slightly before Captain Felch peeks inside. "I'm not here as a captain," he explains. "I'm just a big brother right now."

And right away, Becky bursts into tears again before staggering from her chair across the room so he can engulf her in a hug.

14

ALEXIS

Becky's fingers twist in her lap while her eyes bore holes into her brother. "He's out there somewhere, Chris. What am I supposed to do?"

"The only thing you have to do is wait and let the police do what they do." He brushes loose hair behind her ear before taking her chin in his hand. "I know, it's like asking you to breathe underwater. But you have to try. You have to believe we're doing everything in our power to find him."

And here I am, standing in the corner, quietly observing their interaction and sort of wishing someone would ask me to leave the room. The last thing I want to do is get in the way of a moment like this, yet I'm torn. He isn't supposed to get too close to the case, not as a professional. I want to be sure he doesn't interfere, though my concerns leave me feeling like I'm the interloper.

It's as if he hears me thinking, glancing my way over his shoulder. "Thank you for breaking that up earlier," he murmurs before wincing slightly. "I felt it best to stay out of it. It's hard enough dealing with him when there isn't all this added stress."

I assume he's talking about his soon to be ex brother-in-law. I have no siblings of my own, but I can easily imagine wanting to strangle their partner if that partner cheated on them and left them floundering and working nonstop to make ends meet. Besides, brothers can be very protective, especially older ones.

Captain Felch certainly seems to qualify, hovering over his sister like a worried mother hen. "Have you eaten?" he murmurs.

She shakes her head, waving a hand at his disapproving grunt. "Come on. I couldn't possibly. I can barely swallow coffee, much less eat anything."

"You have to keep your strength up." He may as well be speaking to one of his kids, tender and concerned and protective. "Pete would want you to. You know he would."

"Don't go throwing my kid in my face like that," she warns, though there's a little bit of a smile tugging at the corners of her mouth.

"But it's true," he insists. "Of all people, he would be the first one to make sure you have what you need."

"Something his father should be doing." There is unspeakable pain and betrayal in Becky's voice now. "But no, he's busy pretending he's in his twenties again, knocking up a girl who's barely out of her teens. How could he bring her here?"

"We wanted to question both of them," Captain Felch reminds her. "They do live together. It was important to get an idea of Pete's relationship with both of them, if possible."

It's almost like Becky finally remembers I'm here, looking around her brother to ask, "And did you get an idea of that?"

I might have gotten a better idea had she not interrupted us so suddenly and thoroughly, but telling her so would help no one. "It seems like a typical sort of situation. He feels guilty. He wishes he'd spent more time with Pete."

"He told you that?" she asks, skeptical.

I can only offer a gentle smile before shaking my head. "I inferred it from what he said. He has a lot of guilt, that is for sure."

"Yeah, well, he should." Becky wipes a hand under her eyes. "I know how I must seem. The typical jilted wife, full of bitterness, ready to spew bile everywhere. Please, don't write me off because of that."

"I wouldn't write you off."

"It's just that I want to make sure everybody's doing everything they can." She shoots a pleading look to her brother, who pats her hand.

"This is all about Pete." Rubbing her hand, he looks at me. "I assume you got nothing from them?"

"Respectfully, you can't be part of the investigation. Remember?" It's painful, having to remind him of that.

It seems he feels that pain acutely, judging by the way his features pinch together. "From one person to another. Did you?"

I hate having to shake my head. Granted, it wouldn't make me happy to name Andrew as a suspect, but at least it might point us in a direction we can pursue. At the moment, there is no such direction. "A guilty, scared father, his pregnant girlfriend, there wasn't much more than that."

"Looking at her sets my teeth on edge," Becky mutters. "Rubbing her stomach like she's the first woman to ever give birth. I mean, come on. She doesn't even bother trying to look like she's sorry she broke up our marriage."

Captain Felch surprises me by growling. "It takes two to tango." He's an angry older brother and nothing is going to change his opinion.

"Do you think Andrew is capable of hurting Pete?" I ask.

It surprises me how quickly they answer, and how the answer comes in perfect unison. "No."

After a short, awkward little laugh, Captain Felch explains. "He is not my favorite person. There isn't much I would put past him. But that's one thing he doesn't have in him. He may have been a lousy husband, but he was never an abusive one – as far as I know," he adds, looking to his sister.

She wastes no time shaking her head. "Never. Not in any way. He cheated on me, but until then, I had no complaints. He doesn't even have a temper."

"He certainly seemed to have one earlier, when he was shouting during the interview," I murmur.

"I did my fair share of shouting, too." She arches an eyebrow. "Do you suspect me, too?"

"It's standard questioning," the captain murmurs.

"And I was only kidding – well, not really, but I wasn't completely serious. I was only trying to prove a point. Just because you shout while fighting doesn't mean you're a violent person capable of harming your child." Becky falls silent, but her brow is as arched as ever.

She's sharp. I have to give her that. "Counterpoint," I venture, approaching the table. "You blamed Andrew the second you were in the room. It's my job to find out why you made such accusations. Whether there's a history of violence in the household. Neglect. Anything that might lead to a situation like the one we're now in."

Her jaw ticks, and her gaze brushes over her brother before she stares down at the table. "I didn't mean I thought he would ever hurt Pete. Only that he could have been a more present father. When your son goes missing and you don't know why or who might be behind it, you look for somebody to blame. That's all I was doing." She sounds ashamed of herself now that the dust has settled and she can reflect on what she did and how it looked.

"You did what any parent would do in a situation like this," Captain Felch assures her. It feels better and safer to let him talk his sister through this, since she obviously relaxes in his presence. So long as he doesn't try to butt into the finer points of the case.

Eventually, I have to ask one more question, and the idea of mentioning Brittany leaves me wishing there was any other way of getting the information I need. The woman clearly causes Becky stress. Choosing my words carefully, I murmur, "I didn't get much of a sense of how Brittany felt about Pete, aside from her obvious concern and distress." But was that for Andrew's sake, or for the boy's? "Did Pete ever say anything to you about Brittany?"

Becky's brow furrows right on schedule. "What do you mean?"

"Did he talk about her? Did you ever get a sense of the kind of relationship they have when Pete visits?"

It surprises me when her expression softens. I had expected it to harden, to turn bitter again. "They didn't really have much of a relationship."

"Do you know why? What I mean is, was there a fight that you're aware of? Did they butt heads a lot?"

"Pete? Butt heads with an adult?" The captain wears a fond grin, like the idea is unthinkable. Is he a doting uncle now, or a clear-eyed witness? It pains me not to be able to rely on his version of things, when I've relied so heavily on his good sense until now.

Becky shakes her head firmly enough that her ponytail swings. "He's too respectful for that — even toward her. Believe me, his father would let me know if anybody ever disrespected his precious Brittany." I don't think it would be possible for her to roll her eyes any harder. "But Pete appreciated that Brittany didn't try to get too close to him. She doesn't try to be his stepmother or his friend. I don't know whether she did that out of respect or just because she couldn't care less, but it doesn't matter. I would rather see her be standoffish than try to push herself into Pete's life when he doesn't want her there."

"And … " Oh, boy. Here goes nothing. "How did he feel about the baby?"

She lifts a shoulder, scoffing before returning her gaze to the scarred table. "He wasn't thrilled. Told me he thought it was gross. But he's also fourteen, so there's no telling where his opinions on the matter come from."

On the surface, this looks like a typical broken household. Awkwardness around Dad's new girlfriend, around the idea of a new baby, the whole nine yards. It also looks like Pete has two parents who care about him and only want the best, even if they're too busy wrapped up in their own painful drama at the moment.

None of it points to a reason for a bright, sweet kid to go missing.

15

ALEXIS

What a day, and it's still early.

At least one good thing came of all of the drama and excitement of the McClintocks' visit to the station: I couldn't obsess over Dad while I was busy trying to keep a brawl from erupting. Naturally, though, as soon as Becky is ushered out by her brother, I pull out my phone and check in case I missed something. Would I have felt the phone buzzing in my pants pocket? Certainly, but who knows? Stranger things have happened than a missed call.

I can't hold back a grunt of frustration when I find nothing waiting for me. Right away I'm plunged back into the deep end of my fears, imagining all kinds of ugly, painful scenarios Dad could currently be involved in.

What if it's Tyler? What if Tyler took Pete, too? What if he's decided to rage out of control and create as much havoc as he can? That could very well be the case – he might feel the walls closing in, like I'm on his trail and could catch up to him at any moment. He would want to punish me for that, which would mean causing chaos. Spreading me thin, making sure I can't give him my full attention. He could also be acting like a toddler throwing a tantrum. Stomping his feet and holding his breath.

Though in his case, that sort of behavior translates into kidnappings and slashed tires.

It isn't easy to keep a clear head, in other words. I know I can't attribute every ugly situation to that man, but I can't help it. Especially when the victim in this case sits directly in the sweet spot of Tyler's preferences. A young kid, a good kid, probably the type who'd stop to help somebody whose groceries spilled all over the street or who needs help finding their lost dog. We tell ourselves we would never fall for such an obvious trick, but there's no way to know for sure how we would react in the face of a convincing liar with a track record for evading capture.

I return to my office after the interviews but stare at my laptop for a solid ten minutes before realizing I have no idea what I intended to do when I sat down. My thoughts are scattered, all over the place, and that's not going to help anybody. I need to pull myself together, and fast. I would never forgive myself if I missed something in Pete's case all because I was distracted by my own worries.

Funny how thinking of distractions gets my stomach growling. I was barely able to choke down half an English muffin this morning at Mom's assistance. Silly me, assuming I was up too early to bother her. By the time I emerged from my room, she was already brewing another pot of coffee to replace the one she had already finished drinking before I ever opened my eyes.

What a relief to know Mitch is with her now, so she doesn't have to sit alone with her fears. Of course, I imagined she would have certain feelings for Dad to this day, but I didn't imagine it hitting her like this. I should have at least considered the possibility. She feels things very deeply and always has, even if she doesn't always voice her thoughts. It's rare for her to hold her tongue, but when it comes to her ex-husband, she normally avoids the subject. There's no way of avoiding him now.

In other words, she's just as worried about him as I am, if not more. They're no longer married according to the state of Maine, but feelings don't disappear the second a signature appears on a piece of paper.

There are a few dollar bills in my wallet, and right now the idea of grabbing something cheap from the vending machine seems much easier to stomach than going out somewhere to get food. I want to stay close, too, in case the captain needs anything. He's been there for me through my ups and downs starting from the Camille Martin case through Dad's disappearance. The least I can do is hang around in case he needs me to question someone or search the area around Pete's home.

Mitch would shake his head in disappointment if he knew I was going back and forth between a sleeve of chocolate chip cookies and a packet of peanut butter cracker sandwiches. The crackers seem like a better option, and at least there's a little protein involved – very little, I'm guessing.

I feed a couple of bills into the machine and punch the letter and number for the corresponding slot, and soon a package of crackers is mine. It's a poor replacement for lunch, but it will have to do until I'm able to head back to Mom's later. I have no doubt with her anxiety at an all-time high, she'll have a four-course meal prepared. What else is she going to do, pace the floors and worry herself into a nervous breakdown?

I tear the package with my teeth and pull out one of the little sandwiches on my way back to my office.

Forest of Lies

The station is busier than usual thanks to a recent rash of vandalism around town.

It's no surprise to find a handful of teenagers sitting around, looking sullen while awaiting their parents' arrival before being questioned. One of them even has dark blue spray paint on his hands and jeans — what a coincidence, seeing as how the fresh graffiti I noticed this morning as I rolled down Main Street happened to be the same color.

If there's one thing that doesn't fly here in Broken Hill, it's the defacement of the town's commercial buildings. When tourist dollars play such a big part in the town's success, it means there's an image to uphold.

"Agent Forrest?" I turn at the sound of my name being called, only to find the officer at the front desk waving an arm overhead. "Agent Forrest! I just got a call."

Immediately, Dad's face comes to mind. This might have nothing to do with him, but I can't help the way my heart doubles its rhythm in the time it takes me to reach the desk.

"It's good news," she tells me, patting my arm in something like sympathy when I release a shaky breath. "They found your dad. He's fine."

The room is spinning all of a sudden. I can barely squeak out the words, "Are they sure it's him?"

"Absolutely. They pulled him over on his way back from Green Fork based on the APB description."

"Green Fork?" I recognize the name, but the joyous celebration raging in my head is making it sort of difficult to concentrate. "That's around an hour from here, right?"

I can't believe it. I honestly can't believe it.

Did I fall asleep at my desk? Is this a dream? What a cruel dream it would be, if so. I can taste the peanut butter in my mouth from the crackers, and it's much too vivid to exist only in my imagination. I'm still afraid to believe, since my heart would break if this wasn't real.

The officer's smile hasn't faded. "Exactly. He told the troopers he was visiting a friend out there and forgot to bring his phone charger, so it died."

"He forgot his phone charger?" I have to cover my mouth with one hand or else blurt out laughter so loud, it would probably send every cop in the building rushing my way, thinking I was having a fit or something.

All of this over a forgotten phone charger, which I would imagine has melted down to nothing. The idea of us worrying ourselves to death because he forgot to bring a phone charger on a trip is so typically Dad.

The poor girl looks like she doesn't know whether to be glad for me or concerned. "Are you all right?" she asks as I fight to control my laughter. I must look and sound like I've lost my mind.

"I'm fine," I manage to choke out before another perverse giggle bubbles out of my chest. "I'm sorry, but I have to laugh."

"I bet he'll get a new phone charger for Christmas," she suggests with a grin.

"He'll get ten," I confirm. He's fine. He's really fine.

He also must be devastated, having lost everything but what he took with him on his trip. Just like that, my moment of joy softens into gladness mixed with a heavy dose of concern.

I don't know how to get in touch with him so he'll know where to find me if he wants to. I would imagine he's gone back to the trailer park by now. If he hasn't reached it, he'll be there soon, wanting to see the destruction with his own eyes.

First things first. There's renewed energy in my stride as I cut through the station to head for my office. Captain Felch's door is closed and he's on the phone, rubbing his temples while squinting like his head aches. A brief flash of something close to guilt warms my chest. Here I am, overjoyed, while he worries over the fate of his nephew.

That's how life goes, unfair as it is. For every moment of pain, there's someone in the world experiencing their ultimate joy. Every second of every day.

At the moment, concern for Dad's living situation overrides everything else. As soon as I have my office door closed, I call Mom. "Is there any news?" she asks after answering on the first ring.

"He's fine." And now the laughter I couldn't contain turns to something deeper. There's a flood of emotion threatening to break free in the form of tears, only one of which I can't blink back. It rolls down my cheek as I listen to Mom shout to Mitch, that Dad is okay.

After giving her the rundown, I arrive at the only logical conclusion. "I hate to say it, but he needs somewhere to stay, and I doubt he has the money for an indefinite hotel reservation."

I can practically hear reality land on her head like a ton of bricks. "Oh …" she breathes.

"I really do hate to say it," I repeat. "But I doubt he has many other options. What, is he going to stay with one of his friends in the trailer park? They probably don't have any room for him. And you know how he is. He needs his own space."

"This won't be his space," she sniffs. I can almost see the look on her face as clearly as if she were sitting in front of me with her mouth pursed and her chin lifted. "This is my space now."

It's my turn to rub my temples. "I realize that."

"This is a lot." She releases a weary sigh while I wait for her to crumble. She will – it's inevitable. She's a lot of things, my mother, but uncaring isn't one of them. "You said he's been doing better lately? You know, with his problems?"

Problems which she shared. She is still in recovery and always will be, the way he is. "He's sober," I assure her. "And think of it this way. You can support each other."

"You don't need to pep talk me, young woman."

"Mom," I murmur. "Remember how worried we were just a few minutes ago? This is the best possible outcome. He's alive and well, and in need of just about everything now that it all went up in flames."

"All right, all right. Stop bullying me," she grumbles. "Obviously, we're not going to leave him high and dry. He has nowhere to go. I suppose I can learn to live with him again—for a little while," she's quick to add. As if I need to be reminded.

"Until he's back on his feet," I confirm. "Thank you for this. Oh, wait!" I slap a hand to my forehead. "I still need to get in touch with him somehow."

"I'm going to have to leave that one to you," she announces. "Maybe you can put out another one of those, what are they called? Bulletins?"

"I don't think it has to be that extreme," I decide, shuddering at the thought of making the man deal with being pulled over twice in one day like he's a criminal. "I would imagine he's at the trailer park, trying to find whatever is salvageable. I'll send a squad car out to find him there."

After that, I can only cross my fingers and hope for the best.

16

ALEXIS

"He's going to need clothes, isn't he?" Mom's question doesn't seem as though it was directed at me. She's talking to herself, darting around the house like a hummingbird on the loose. "I think there are clothes up in the closet. Maybe the attic…"

"Do you need me to go up and look for you?" Mitch is in the kitchen, wearing a flour-stained apron while something heavenly bakes in the oven. At least, I assume it's heavenly, since it smells that way.

"No, no, you worry about that brioche!" She's already upstairs. I swear, the woman is a living, believing wonder. Her own power generator.

Mitch and I turn to each other. He wipes his hands on the apron before holding his arms out. "Hi. How are you holding up?"

Stepping into his warm embrace is a gift. It loosens my shoulders and my neck, dissolving the tension, easing my worries. "Am I insane?" I whisper, linking my hands behind his back.

"Is that a question, or an update as to how you're feeling?"

"A question." I pull back far enough to look up into his warm, sparkling eyes. There's a little flour on the bridge of his nose which I brush off while sighing. "Having Dad stay here. It's a recipe for disaster."

"For one thing, you aren't forcing anyone to do anything. For another, if she didn't think she could handle it, she would have refused."

If only it were that easy. "There was no way for her to refuse. He has nowhere else to stay."

He tips his head to the side, frowning a little while taking this in. "When it comes to family, you do what you have to do. It doesn't matter whether you think you can handle it or not, you just ... do it."

"They aren't family anymore," I fret.

"Sure, they are," he reminds me, smiling gently as he strokes my cheek and probably leaves flour there. Not that I mind. I sort of like the idea of having a visual reminder of his caress.

"What really matters is he's safe and sound." I have to remind myself of that even as I hear Mom

Forest of Lies

overhead, her rapid foot falls moving back and forth across the ceiling above us.

Mitch chuckles, looking up. "You think this is bad? You should have seen her before we knew he's okay. I was afraid she was going to ask me to help rearrange the furniture. She needed something to do."

I follow him over to the large bowl sitting on the counter, draped with a dish towel. He pulls it aside to reveal a dome of risen dough, studded with raisins by the looks of it. "What is that?" I whisper as my stomach growls. I never did finish those crackers.

"This is going to be cinnamon raisin bread. Two loaves." While he turns the dough onto the counter, I snag a banana from the fruit bowl and scarf it down greedily.

I catch him looking my way as he mixes cinnamon and brown sugar together to spread on the rolled out dough. "Let me guess. You barely ate today."

"I didn't have an appetite."

I know which direction his thoughts have gone in as soon as he lifts an eyebrow. "I'll have to take you home and feed you later."

"I thought you were going to feed me here." I wave a hand, indicating the loaves he's rolling up and plopping into loaf pans. "What, is that not for me?"

"One of them could be, if you play your cards right," he teases with a grin. "But the idea was to leave them here for your mom. Who knows? Maybe she and your dad will share cinnamon raisin bread and decide they're in love again."

"Maybe we'll what?" Mom's voice rings out from the hall.

I can barely bite back a laugh as Mitch's face goes red. "She's not just fast. She's silent when she feels like it," I whisper while he chokes.

He manages to clear his throat before offering, " I was only trying to get Alexis to laugh."

"That's what you get for teasing me," I tell him before giggling again at his sour expression.

That giggle is cut off by the ringing of the doorbell. My heart jumps into my throat before I can jump off the stool by the counter. "I'll get it!" I shout, already halfway down the hall. On the other side of the curtain covering the glass, I see someone waiting on the porch. Nothing in the world matters more than throwing my arms around my dad right now. I was so sure I had lost him.

When I fling the door open, his anxious expression brings me up short. "Dad," I breathe, touching a hand to my chest. "You're really here. You're all right."

He blinks rapidly, his jaw ticking while his eyes dart around over my shoulder. "I haven't... Not since..."

Oh. I hadn't thought of this. That's so unlike me, too. Normally, I work out every possibility well in advance. I have already imagined Mom and Dad somehow simultaneously strangling each other to death, but I didn't think about this. What it would be like for him to re-enter his old home, somewhere he sank countless hours and effort into when he lived here. When there were four of us.

"There's been some changes," I whisper, holding out my hands. "But it's the same place. And you're welcome here. Now please, would you let me give you a hug already?"

All of my reassurance isn't enough to ease his worries. The shaky sigh he releases before stepping over the threshold tells me so. But once he sets his bag on the floor and I get my arms around him, it doesn't matter. I have him. He's still here.

"Thank you for still being alive," I whisper in his ear, choked by tears. "I was so scared. You don't leave the house without at least two phone chargers from now on."

"Deal," he murmurs, patting my back.

"Mr. Forrest." Mitch joins us, without the apron this time, and shakes Dad's hand. "We were all pretty worried about you. I'm so sorry for what happened."

"It's like I'm dreaming, but I can't wake up," Dad admits. "Everything's gone. I went over there, and it's all ... just gone." He wears the vague, faraway expression of someone who's trying to function while fighting to catch up to reality at the same time.

"I am so sorry," I whisper once I've gotten my emotions under control. "You know if you need any help, I'm here. I'll do everything I can."

His mouth twists into a familiar smirk as he studies the bright, white walls of the entry hall. It's a far cry from the old-fashioned wallpaper that once covered them. "I think you've already done enough, convincing your mother to let me stay here. How did you manage it?"

"Why don't you ask me that question yourself?" Mom emerges from the kitchen, and profound silence descends. I'm fairly sure I can hear the bread rising in the oven while the two of them exchange a long look.

Dad speaks first. "Hello. Thank you for this."

Mom offers a slight nod. "Of course. I was sorry to hear about your misfortune."

"My misfortune?" To my surprise, he snorts. "Come on. We can loosen up a little. My home burned down. It wasn't much, but it was mine. And now it's gone."

"Hey." I rub his shoulder, feeling a little awkward thanks to the way his voice trembles a little. "It could've been worse. You could've been inside. Things can be replaced. And like I said— "

"I know. Whatever I need." His tone is withering, to say the least, but there's the ghost of a smile behind it. "Thank you."

Mom slowly approaches, her gaze trained on the bag Dad left on the floor. "Is that all you have now?"

He looks at the bag, then at her. "It seems that way."

"Good thing I kept some of your clothes upstairs." She folds her arms and looks him up and down before nodding. "You're about the same size. Maybe a little thinner. I guess without somebody to do the cooking for you, there's no chance of putting on a few extra pounds."

"Is there anything else you would like to point out? Is kicking a man when he's down a hobby you picked up recently?"

They have been under the same roof for three minutes, and already the tension is beginning to build. I shoot Mitch a worried look, but he seems unconcerned. I suppose that's easy for him. They aren't his parents. He has no memory of the way things used to be in the good days, back when they didn't look at each other with wariness and mistrust.

"I'm only trying to make sure you have what you need," Mom tells him. "It's been a long time since we've seen each other, and I want to catch up. Make sure you're taken care of."

"You don't owe me a thing. And I've been taking care of myself for a long time now."

"Which is why you've lost weight," she points out. At least there's the beginnings of a grin stirring at the corners of her mouth. They could be at this all night, arguing in circles until one of them drops.

Finally, Mitch clears his throat. "Well, the brioche is cooling on the counter, and there are two loaves of bread in the oven. When the timer goes off, you'll need to take them out." I'm surprised to find him already pulling his coat from the peg on the wall "I'm going to take Alexis here to get something to eat before she keels over. I assume everything is okay here?" He looks from one of them to the other and back again.

"Sure," Mom decides. "Everything is fine here. You two run along."

I'm a little confused, but then this has been a confusing sort of day. Dad gives me another quick hug – but fierce. "Take care of yourself," he murmurs before pressing a kiss against my temple. "Your old mom and dad can handle it. Focus on you tonight."

"I'll do my best." Though no matter what, there's going to be part of me waiting to hear about a domestic disturbance call to this address. I give them all of an hour before Mom says something to set him off, or Dad comments on the renovations she's made. Considering the way the tension crackles as we're leaving, it feels inevitable.

But they're both safe. Right now, I need to focus on the things that are going right.

17

ALEXIS

"It's a good thing you've left so much of your stuff here." Mitch reaches into a drawer in his dresser and, to my surprise, pulls out a pair of yoga pants, and sweatshirt I recognize as my own. "I've made it a point to keep them together for whenever you might need them."

"I didn't realize I left so much here." Peeking into the drawer, I find another two pairs of pants, along with a couple of T-shirts. "I have an official drawer in your dresser?" I can't help but smile at the sweetness.

He plays it off in his usual, unruffled manner. "I figured it was better than keeping a laundry basket around to trip over every time I walk into the room." Even though he's joking, he gives me a quizzical look. "Is that all right?"

Forest of Lies

"Of course!" Poor thing. He looked genuinely worried. I have to give him a hug, though I'm still chuckling as I do. "It's great. Thank you. I don't know what I would do without you."

"You would figure something out." After kissing the top of my head, he tilts it back to look me in the eye. "You were doing a pretty good job before we got back together, right?"

That's the thing. I barely remember. I thought I was doing all right, certainly. I had my work, which for a long time was enough to sustain me. Rather, that was what I told myself.

I also hardly had a relationship with Mom, hadn't seen my father in years, and had been branded undateable by just about every man I attempted a relationship with. Things would always start out well enough, but once the guy in question figured out I wasn't kidding when I talked about unpredictable hours and how there was no guarantee I'd be able to keep the plans we made in advance, things would inevitably fizzle out.

Why is it so many people have a hard time believing a person when they flat-out tell the truth? Maybe those guys thought they were special. That I hadn't yet found the man capable of making me forget my job.

Mitch isn't like that. As I slip into clean, comfortable clothes after such an emotionally trying day with the promise of pizza and beer for dinner, I don't think I've ever been so grateful for him.

By the time I join him in the living room, the pizza has been delivered and is sitting open on the coffee table. The heavenly aroma of cheese and pepperoni hang in the air, making my mouth water. "This looks nice," I offer as I take a seat. "What did you get for yourself?"

"If you ate this entire large, extra cheese pepperoni pizza by yourself ... I wouldn't even be mad," he decides, cracking open a beer and handing it over. "I'd be pretty impressed, if anything."

"I'll be generous and let you have some, too." After snagging a slice and taking a bite, my eyes close so I can fully experience the delicious flavors dancing over my tongue. "Oh, man. That is good."

"Does it hit the spot?"

"Most definitely. Thank you." With the large slice balanced on a paper plate, I settle back against the cushions with a weary sigh. "What a day. I'm happy but I don't have the energy to show it."

"Understandable. Maybe a little food will perk you up, though. Everything's all right. You can sleep easier tonight." For a moment, his words loosen the hand clenched around my heart. It's still there, even knowing Dad is safe – at least relatively, considering he still has to contend with Mom.

"I can't stop thinking about that family. Felch's nephew," I admit. "I'm supposed to get a call as soon as anybody learns anything, and since the phone hasn't rung yet, I can only assume the kid is still missing."

"That's a shame," Mitch agrees, solemnly. "But you can't solve the world's problems."

"Oh, I know. But the captain's been so nice and supportive. I really want this to work out well for his family."

"Of course. Hopefully, it will." By now, he's already polished off a slice and is reaching for another. He hesitates, though, lifting an eyebrow and looking at me before snagging it. "Am I allowed?"

"Knock it off." We're both laughing by the time we start off on our second slices, and he was right. I do feel better now that I've got a little food in me. It might not be the healthiest option, but it's delicious and hot and much more substantial than a pack of crackers or a banana.

I angle myself until I'm facing him, one leg tucked under the other. "How was your day?" I ask. "We always talk too much about me."

"Oh, you know how it is. Baking while a frantic woman pretended she wasn't frantic. Things could've been worse." He manages to swallow before laughing. "Your mom was wondering if I offer lessons."

"What, in baking?"

"Yeah, I had to tell her I'm not really at that level ... yet." He wiggles his eyebrows. "Maybe someday."

"Well, you know how I feel about it. Keep honing your craft and I'll be more than happy to sample the outcome."

"So that's how it is, huh?" He shakes his head in mock disappointment, clicking his tongue. "You think this is all about free baked goods?"

"What else could it be about?" I tease. "I mean, let's be fair. You have the enviable job of taking care of me, putting up with my crazy hours, making sure I'm fed. You even take care of my family. The least you can do is treat me to delicious pastries and breads."

"What do I get for it?" he asks, setting his plate aside.

"I thought I just described it for you. The pleasure of taking care of me." Somehow I manage to maintain a straight face as I put my plate aside, then climb into his lap with one leg on either side of his before I settle in facing him, arms wrapped around his neck. "But if that isn't enough, maybe we can work something out."

"What did you have in mind?" The touch of his hands on my hips is beyond welcome. That simple contact, the intimacy of it. No matter what happens out there, at the end of the day we have this. That's why I can't in good conscience claim I had everything together before I came back here. Even when I was dating, even when the relationships were new and fresh and exciting, there was never anything like this. A connection deeper than the physical. This man sees me. He knows me. He understands me – and what's more, he wants to understand.

He's also my refuge. My escape. At the moment, that's what I need. To forget about Mom and Dad for a minute and let them handle their things on their own. I need to forget about the McClintocks, and even about Captain Felch. What is it they say? You can't pour water from an empty cup.

Now, I need to fill my cup, which means placing a soft, featherlight kiss against Mitch's lips. He tastes like pepperoni and tomato sauce — not a bad combination. Not even close. "How's that for a first payment?" I ask, brushing my nose against his.

"Not bad, but I might need a second installment. You know, to show me you're serious." His eyes twinkle enchantingly. I could get lost in them, could drown in those baby blue depths.

"Let me leave no doubt about it." This time, the kiss is deep and firm and long, so long we're both breathing harder by the time we come up for air.

"Hmm." His hands slide up and down my back, sending fiery sizzles through the rest of me. "Interesting."

"What do you mean?" My fingers thread through his hair as I speak, something I know he loves.

"It seems like you're fairly committed to repayment. That was an impressive installment."

"I do my best."

After another kiss, which leads to a second, and then a third, he lets me up for air again. I don't want to be let up for air, though – my body takes over for me, and I lean in again, expecting the touch of his lips. He merely chuckles teasingly. "What about dinner?" he murmurs with a faint but incredibly interesting little growl in his voice.

"It just so happens, you've woken up my other appetites. It's all your fault," I tell him, wiggling a little in his lap until he groans.

"And there I was, about to suggest we find time to get away as soon as possible. As much as I love making out with you on my couch, there's something to be said for a change in scenery." He reaches up to tuck a strand of hair behind my ear, then lets his fingers trail down my cheek in a soft caress. "Besides, you could use a getaway."

I love the idea. It lights me up inside and makes my heart swell. However ... "I wish I could guarantee exactly when that could happen." I have to whimper in frustration as I touch my forehead to his. "I really wish somebody would make up their mind at the Bureau. This whole business of living in limbo is starting to grate on my nerves."

"You're not alone in that. I would sort of like to know where my girlfriend will be calling home in the future."

"Still, that doesn't mean we can't make it work. Right?" I find myself searching his familiar face for a sign of agreement.

I think I could fall in love with the lines at the corners of his eyes that always come out when he smiles. "Are you kidding? Making it work is what we do."

In a flash, though, his hands tighten around my hips and pull me closer. "We do a lot of other things, too. Some of which I would like to get down to right now."

"Mitch Dutton," I whisper, winding my arms around his neck again, "I love the way you think."

18

KILLER

I'm a man who's accustomed to being disappointed.

People have disappointed me my entire life. I'm sure any therapist would have a field day, connecting the dots of my past. Drawing conclusions, making up stories to explain why I do what I do. Why I am who I am. Someone so entirely beyond the painfully boring, achingly predictable sheep surrounding him.

Because I am so often disappointed. When just about everybody I know lets me down, it's a rare thing to find someone who engages my interest and holds it. I could count on one hand the number of people who have lived in my memory for more than a day, a week, a month.

That's why Madeline still lives in my memory. So bright and vivid. I can almost feel her frantic little breaths against my hand once I had clamped it over her mouth to stifle screams she never had the chance to release. The light, enticingly floral scent of her hair. The sound of her voice, still so clear after the hours upon hours we spent talking. When she told me everything there was to know about her sweet little life. Even the fact that she fought for her life at the end makes her special. She didn't give up, even to her final breath. She fought, because she had something worth fighting for.

Until now, her kid sister has kept me engaged. She's clever and determined. Like a dog going after a bone. There is no swaying her once she sets her mind to something—in that respect, we are very much alike. I'm determined, as well.

Still, I hoped she would take my message for what it was. That she would see my only intention was to get a rise out of her. To find out whether she would jump at the bait I was dangling in front of her face.

What, did she think I was stupid enough to go to her mom's house? She's a woman who's been living on that block for decades. Everybody knows everybody. And from what I've observed of her while following her routine, she is quite social.

She has a lot of acquaintances – after all, she is the woman whose daughter was murdered, and whose husband went away for attempted murder not long after. In other words, she's a celebrity in a town as small and quiet as Broken Hill.

I wouldn't be surprised if her neighbors keep an eye out for her because of that.

The former convict, though? The one who lives in a trailer park? It's much easier to create a little mischief in a place like that. Especially when you know the homeowner is out of town.

The way I see it, there was no harm done. Not really. I only watched from a distance, but it was clear the pitiful little structure went up in no time. I was out of there long before the first truck reached the scene, but it was already too late for them to do anything about it. I mean, if anything, I did the man a favor. Hopefully he'll find someplace better. He might even get insurance money out of the fire to start a new life.

Though the idea does leave me wincing as I make another slow ride past Mitch's house. I don't dare park nearby, and this will be the last time I drive past tonight. He'll be more guarded now – for all I know, he might install a camera to keep watch outside the house. I can't afford to make it easy to identify me. I just needed one more look. Confirmation of Alexis' whereabouts.

Forest of Lies

The fact is, I didn't exactly go out of my way to cover my tracks when I set that fire. Arson isn't my normal choice of recreation. I don't know the first thing about making it look less suspicious.

When I think about it while driving away from Mitch's block, I have to admit to myself, if no one else, that I could have put a little more effort into making it look accidental. After all, I've been covering my tracks for decades, and no one has come anywhere close to identifying me ... until Alexis came along, but then she's special.

And we do have a bond, don't we? If I were the sort of man who believed in a higher power, or some great, invisible hand of fate, I would think we are forever attached because of Madeline. That she is the thin, golden thread holding us together. That could be why Alexis has been the only one to come this close to me yet. It could also be why, though I know she's on to me, I can't bring myself to leave. Normally, if this were anybody else, I would pull up stakes and find a new life elsewhere. Start over, inevitably get bored, then begin my recreational activities all over again. That's how it's gone over and over, after all. Sometimes there are months between hunts, sometimes years.

When I check in with my gut and ask it whether or not it's time to go, the idea never fails to set my teeth on edge. I feel no urgency, no breath on the back of my neck. Sure, she's come close, but her boring predictability grants me a measure of comfort. I'm disappointed in her penchant for falling for my tricks, but it works in my favor.

What next? I mull over the question during my drive, humming along to the oldies on the radio. It's a cold, quiet night, the sort of night that drives people into the warmth and comfort of their homes. They exist in their little bubbles, glad to be out of the cold. Unaware of the predator driving past their glowing windows.

There was a time when a night like this would make for ideal hunting. That's how I've come to think about it. Stalking my prey. Luring them in. Waiting until the last moment to reveal myself.

Alone in the truck, I entertain a shiver of pleasure at the thought. It's one of my favorite aspects of my work. Drawing out the tension. Sensing the shift in the air when they begin to suspect I have the wrong intentions. That perhaps they should never have accepted a ride or strayed too close to my vehicle. That the kindly, warm man who asked for help or offered it might not be all he pretends.

Nowadays, people are savvier. Even kids. Too many of them are jaded enough to ignore a stranger rolling up beside them and offering a ride on a frigid night. They know too much about the world thanks to social media. It makes my work more challenging, but in a way it adds to the satisfaction of capturing my latest conquest. Knowing I located the ideal candidate, someone easily lured into the spider's web.

My thoughts stray once again to Alexis as I drive further from the heart of town. She's breathing a sigh of relief tonight, no doubt. The pieces of her life are back in place. I think I'll let her soak in that feeling for a little while, until she begins letting her guard down again. I'm always on her mind–I know her well enough to know that with absolute certainty–but I won't be at the forefront.

Until I announce myself again.

Next time, things might not turn out so well in the end. I still haven't decided whether or not to go through with my threats to her loved ones. There are pros and cons on both sides. Heightened danger, higher stakes.

For now, it's enough to know I hold her parents' well-being in my hands. Her boyfriend's, too. That I and I alone have the power to decide just how they'll live out what's left of their lives.

By the time Main Street is in the rearview mirror, I'm whistling like a man on top of the world.

19

BENJI

Were the police ever going to do anything?

Benji's eyes were still tired and a little raw when he woke up the first Saturday morning after Pete disappeared. It wasn't easy to sleep, knowing your best friend was out there somewhere . Lost and cold, maybe. Afraid. Alone.

Benji wasn't stupid. He knew real life didn't go the way it did on TV. Cases weren't solved immediately. There wasn't a big moment where everything fell into place all at once, the way it happened on TV shows. It would take time.

But how much time? That was the problem. Maybe not everything that happened on TV was real, but one thing had to be true, there was a certain number of

Forest of Lies

hours the police had to find somebody before things got really bad. Like, there might not even be a chance to find him at all now that it had taken so long.

There was nothing in the whole world worse than sitting back and feeling helpless. Somebody had to do something, but the people with that power weren't getting anywhere. Every hour that went by was another hour Pete hadn't been found. And every hour meant there was a little less chance of finding him.

He had to do something.

Once he made up his mind, he jumped out of bed and got through his chores as fast as he could. He made his bed, made sure all of his dirty clothes and towels were in the hamper and left it by his bedroom door, then got in the shower and dressed in warm clothes after that. Looking for Pete would probably mean being outside most of the day, and as usual, it was cold out. There had been a little bit of snow overnight, but not so much that he wouldn't be able to walk around town and maybe go down to the river where he and Pete had hung out a few times. He was starting to get desperate. He didn't want to overlook anything.

He went downstairs, where his mom was in the kitchen, making breakfast. As usual, she sort of frowned when she saw him. Like she was sad, like she felt sorry for him. "How are you doing today?" she asked in a soft voice. "Did you sleep all right?"

"I slept fine." He didn't want to get into all this talking stuff. It was too uncomfortable, and besides, he didn't know how to explain the way he felt. Even if he could, he knew she would probably tell him he was too young to do anything about Pete or to maybe find him. Moms were like that. They wanted to help, but sometimes they could smother a guy a little bit.

"Be sure to eat up. I made plenty." She pulled a tray of pancakes from the oven and added the ones she had just finished cooking before leaving the tray on the counter. His appetite had been fine, even though it seemed like his mom sort of expected it not to be. He especially wanted to be sure to eat a lot since he didn't know how long he would be out, or whether he would come back home for lunch.

"What are you planning on doing today?" She sat down across from him with a cup of coffee and a couple of pancakes. If anything, it seemed like she had trouble eating lately. Like she was upset, even though she tried hard to hide it behind a smile. "Maybe we could go see a movie?"

"Where's Dad?" he asked, glancing at the coffee mug next to the sink.

"He had to go into the office for a little bit, but he'll be back around lunchtime. Maybe the three of us could go out together," she suggested. It wasn't that they didn't normally spend time together, because they did. They did lots of things together, even when there were times Benji would have rather stayed home and played a game or read a book. But nowadays, since Pete went missing, they were on his back all the time. Wanting to make sure he never felt lonely, always asking if there was anything he wanted to talk about. They were doing their best, and he knew it, but it was a little too much after only a couple of days.

He shrugged and did his best not to roll his eyes. He didn't want to hurt her feelings, but there were more important things to worry about. "I don't know. I was kind of thinking of going out by myself for a little while. I won't go far," he promised when his mother frowned. "And I'll be real careful, and my phone is fully charged. I sort of wanted to go down to the park and other places where we would sometimes hang out."

He got the reaction he expected, but then he didn't want to lie, either. "Oh, sweetie," she murmured with the kind of look on her face that meant she felt sorry for him and maybe even wanted to cry a little bit. "Honey, you're not going to find him there. The police have already combed the area."

"I'm not looking for Pete." He sounded a little angrier than he meant to, so he took a breath before adding, "I just wanted to, you know. Be someplace we used to go together. Like I said, I won't be long. I'll definitely be home for dinner."

"It's cold out there." She sounded worried, which made sense. She was probably thinking about Mrs. McClintock, and how awful it was to have a kid go missing. He wanted to tell her he was smart enough not to get himself kidnapped, but that would have been unfair to Pete. Pete was smart, too, smarter than Benji. And look what happened to him.

"I'll wear my scarf and hat, and I'll keep my coat zipped. I'll be fine." He finished off the rest of his pancakes and gulped down orange juice before getting up and washing his things in the sink. The sooner he got out, the better.

It was cold, even colder now that there was a coating of snow on the ground. The wind blew over it and turned the air downright icy, making him tighten his scarf and tuck his chin inside the cocoon it made around his neck. It would probably warm up a little as the day went on—it was still early, and clouds were starting to break up, meaning the sun would come out. Shoving his gloved hands into his pockets, he started out, walking down the long driveway.

As he continued on away from their development, he racked his brain for any memories of things Pete mentioned to him about where he liked to go on his own. There had been times – especially when his parents were still living together and fighting all the time, before Mr. McClintock moved out – that Pete had escaped the house, taking a book with him. Sometimes, he went to the park that sat between their houses, almost equally distant from both of them. They used to meet up there sometimes since it was right in the middle.

He went there first, walking fast, keeping his head down. What was he going to find? He had no idea. He only knew he had to try. The park was empty, a little sad looking. A stiff breeze made the swings sway, and it was pretty creepy when the chains rattled and squeaked. He was freaking himself out over nothing – he looked around in all directions and found nobody nearby. Eventually he left and walked into town to visit the bookstore and the game store where they would sometimes visit and watch D&D games. All it did was remind him how much he missed his friend. There were maybe ten times since Pete went missing that Benji had picked up his phone, ready to call him, before remembering Pete wouldn't be home.

He was starting to get tired by the time he was near the river, and the sun that had come out was starting to slip down lower in the sky. Still, he kept walking. He didn't stop until he reached the river, and for a while, all he did was stand and listen to the water flowing past. Hunger was starting to stir in his belly – he checked his phone and saw that it was already 3:30. No wonder the light had changed, going all warm and amber. It wouldn't be long until dark. Maybe it would be better to go home now.

But he had already come so far, and he wasn't far away from what Pete called "the cave". They had gone there before to hang out, sometimes bringing fishing poles, sometimes throwing rocks into the water while they talked about nothing all that important. A flash of regret stabbed him in the chest. What he wouldn't give to waste time with Pete again.

It wasn't a cave, really. Only an overhang sticking out from a wall of rock that provided a little roof for whoever sat underneath it. Right on the banks of the river, where the water was higher than usual thanks to all the melting snow from the past week or two. He was careful where he stepped, going slowly until he reached the spot.

What did he expect? He must've expected something, or else his heart wouldn't sink as he looked around at the snow-covered rocks. Footprints, maybe. It was clear nobody had been there recently—at least, not since the snow fell overnight. Pete wasn't there.

He let out a single, frustrated groan before something caught his eye. Something that fluttered a little when the breeze blew through. He crouched, digging at loose rocks on the ground, before he was able to pull out a book.

This time, he laughed out loud. The Hobbit. Of course, this would be here. He could imagine Pete sitting there, reading by flashlight if it was dark, letting himself get sucked into another world. But would he have left it? That was the question.

Inside, there was a folded paper. That was what had caught his eye, sticking halfway out of the pages. He pulled it free and unfolded it carefully.

A drawing. Dinosaurs. Pete had been into dinosaurs lately, drawing them, trying to perfect their scaly skin.

What made Benji's hands shake was the memory of watching Pete doodle it in art class the day before he disappeared.

He folded it up and tucked it back into the book, which he shoved into his pocket before setting off again. He wasn't planning on going home anymore.

He was going to the police station.

20

ALEXIS

It's starting to get dark outside the windows by the time I sit back in my chair, rolling my head from side to side in a vain attempt to loosen the tension that's built up over hours spent in front of my laptop. Captain Felch pulled a few strings and called in a few favors, and I've spent hours poring over every detail of the photos taken at what is left of Dad's trailer. What am I looking for? I have no idea. I only know that, according to the captain's friend at the fire department, they're leaning toward calling it arson.

I can only think of one person in the entire world who would deliberately burn down my father's trailer, and imagining Tyler coming so close to my family makes me sick to my stomach. This isn't a case of jumping to conclusions – if anything, I've gone out of my way to avoid connecting Tyler to the fire in the days since it burned.

He's my only viable suspect, though. That's the problem. The questions I asked around the trailer park today confirmed what I already knew; everybody loves my dad. He is everybody's best friend, helpful, dependable. They miss him over there. After giving them time to think things over, the neighbors still can't recall seeing or hearing anything out of the ordinary in the early morning hours before the trailer went up in smoke. There's a dead end squarely in front of me, a brick wall, and the frustration is crushing.

In other words, I need to take my mind off this for a little bit. I'm getting nowhere and frustrating myself worse with every passing hour.

Maybe I should go over and make sure Mom and Dad haven't killed each other yet. Granted, there haven't been any calls from either of them to tip me off to any problems, but still. They might want to avoid worrying me. The fact that they are both grown adults capable of handling their business occurs to me, but I still feel a strange sense of responsibility. No, I did not burn down my father's home. No, there's no way of knowing for sure who did – at least, not yet. Maybe soon, but not yet.

At the end of the day, it was my idea that he stay with Mom. I don't want her resenting me for it if all they've managed to do is bicker.

Once I've got my coat on, I grab my bag and turn off the light in my office. Captain Felch's office is dark, the blinds pulled over the windows. He finally went home for a little while at his wife's insistence, though I'm sure Pete is never far from his mind no matter where he happens to be. There's still not so much as a faint lead in the case. Deputies have interviewed just about everybody in the kid's life, from his teachers to his few friends. Everybody tells the same story of a good kid who had never been any trouble to anyone. The sort of kid you never worry about, because he always manages to handle himself.

He's on my mind as I walk through the station, raising my hand to say good night to the handful of officers at their desks. I want nothing more than a cup of hot tea and something sweet to go with it after the day I've had. I wouldn't mind spending a little time with my favorite baker while I'm at it.

I would leave the station and head over to Mitch's store if it wasn't for what I notice in one of the molded plastic chairs by the station entrance. He can't be older than his early teens, all knees and elbows and wide eyes. A slight smattering of acne across his forehead peeks out from beneath his knit hat. "Are you waiting for somebody?" I ask him, coming to a stop in front of where he's sitting.

Forest of Lies

"No. I mean, I don't know," he admits. "I wanted to talk to somebody about my friend. Pete McClintock. His uncle is a captain and I figured I could talk to him, but he's not here."

"Well, my name is Alexis." I lower myself into a chair beside him. "Maybe I can help you."

"Are you even a cop?" He looks me up and down, probably confused to find me without a uniform.

"Something like that. I work for the FBI, and I've been trying to help with Pete's disappearance. What's your name?"

"Benji. Pete's my best friend."

Right away, I recognize the name. It was the first one to tumble from Becky's lips when she listed the people Pete was closest to aside from his family. From what I remember, the two of them are pretty much cut from the same cloth, both into fantasy books and video games. A little nerdy, maybe, but a good kid.

I give him my warmest smile, hoping to ease his nerves. "Hi, Benji. What can I do for you?"

He reaches into his coat pocket, and I hold my breath until I see he's withdrawing a book. "I went looking around today," he explains. "You know, places Pete and I would hang out, places he liked to hang out by himself sometimes. I thought, I don't know. Maybe it would help."

"Where did you go?" I ask, eyeing the book. The Hobbit. Yes, that sounds like something Pete would be into.

"The park between our houses, a couple other places around town. And then I decided to go down to the river."

"That might've been dangerous. It's pretty cold out, too."

"Yeah, I know, but … " He looks down at the book, tapping his thumbs against the cover. "I don't know. I felt like I had to do something."

He holds the book out to me. "I found this hidden under some rocks. There's a drawing inside." When I don't immediately take it, he thrusts it my way. I wish he had left the book where it was. By now, his fingerprints are all over it, and he could very well have wiped away any prints from a perpetrator – if this is, indeed, evidence.

I hold up a finger before reaching into my coat for a pair of latex gloves. "I tend to carry them with me," I explain, pulling them on before taking the book in my hands. "Just in case."

There is a folded piece of paper sticking out from between the pages, almost like a bookmark. "It's the drawing," Benji explains in a voice tight with either fear or excitement. "I saw him drawing that. We have art class together. He drew it the day before he disappeared."

Dinosaurs. He drew dinosaurs. He's not a bad artist, either, at least for a kid his age. "Are you absolutely sure this is what you saw Pete drawing that day?" I ask, looking up into the boy's troubled eyes.

He wets his lips with the tip of his tongue. "Yeah. I know that's what he was working on that day. We had some free time at the end of class, and he was kind of doodling, you know? I know he drew it that day."

Which means Pete was by the river sometime between drawing this and vanishing. "Was he in the habit of storing books in hiding places outside the house?" I ask, turning it over in my hands. It looks fairly clean except for a few dirty smudges, and the edges of the pages are slightly wrinkled thanks to moisture.

I swallow back the lump in my throat and make it a point not to look at Benji, worried he'll see my concerns written across my face. Though I wouldn't admit it out loud, the fact that we have yet to find anything related to Pete's case is not a good sign. I hate thinking that way, but any law enforcement officer who's been on the job more than a few minutes knows the more time that passes, the less likely we are to find a living victim.

It could be if Pete was murdered, his killer might have hidden the book there to remove any trace of the kid's presence. They wouldn't want to keep the book on them, either, since it might raise suspicions. They would want to dispose of any evidence, and hiding it under some rocks by the river might have seemed like a surefire way to avoid discovery.

Until I have any further evidence, though, this is nothing but conjecture. "Can you show me the place where you found this?" I ask while tucking the drawing between the pages once again, then signaling to a passing officer. "Can I get an evidence bag?" I murmur, and a moment later he presents me with one.

"You think this might mean something?" Benji's eyes are as big as saucers as he watches me slide the book into the bag.

"It might. And there might be other things in the area you aren't trained to look for," I explain as evenly and casually as I can. "Can you take me there?"

"Sure. I know exactly where it is." There's color in his cheeks when he jumps to his feet. "I can take you there right now."

Glancing toward the glass doors, I see how quickly darkness is falling. Should we wait until tomorrow? Could evidence be destroyed overnight if I do?

The idea helps me make up my mind. "Let's go. I'll drive us."

21

ALEXIS

"Do you have a cell?" It's probably a silly question, since Benji is Pete's age and most kids have a cell nowadays by the time they're teenagers.

"Yeah." He unzips one of his pockets and pulls out an iPhone.

"Do me a favor and call your parents," I tell him, driving us along the route Benji outlined on the way to the car. "Let them know where you are, that you're with an FBI agent, and that I will drive you home once you finish showing me where you found this."

Poor kid. I can hear him gulp. "My mom is probably going to be mad. She doesn't want me going out and looking for Pete, you know? It's sad that she doesn't care. She likes Pete – everybody does."

"I'm sure she doesn't want you to take chances and get yourself into trouble," I tell him as we come to a stop at a red light. "So yes, she might be a little annoyed with you, but it's not because she doesn't care about Pete. Things like this happen, parents start to wonder how they would feel if it were their kid who went missing. Don't be too hard on her."

"Now tell her not to be too hard on me." He's laughing humorlessly as he places the call. Right away, I hear a loud, almost shrill voice on the other end. No doubt she wants to know where he's been all day.

"I know," he mumbles. "I know. No, I'm not coming home right now, but I will be. I'm with this FBI lady."

"Agent Forrest," I call out for her benefit.

"Right," Benji tells her. "Agent Forrest. I found something that belongs to Pete, and she wants me to show her where I found it. But she's going to drive me home when we're finished." He pauses, then sighs heavily. "I guess if I'm gonna be safe with anybody, it would be with an FBI agent. Right?"

Once the call is over, he releases a shaky sigh. "She's real mad."

"She's worried. I would be, too."

"Because there's somebody out there taking kids?" I hear the slight tremor in his voice. How vulnerable it must make him feel.

"I mean in general. I didn't want to give you the idea you have anything to be afraid of. Still," I add lightly, "it never hurts to be careful. Aware of your surroundings. You might think it's no big deal to go off someplace with somebody you don't know because they seem friendly and normal. But the kind of people who would take kids work really, really hard to make themselves seem normal. They want to be trusted. I'm not trying to scare you," I promise when a glance his way reveals wide, fearful eyes. "But it's good to be on the safe side."

"I guess you see lots of, like, cases like this."

It's no surprise when Maddie's face floats in front of me. "I've seen a few," I murmur, pulling into the woods lining the riverbank at Benji's direction. The shadows are getting deeper with every passing minute, and the sky has taken on the particular shade of lilac and gray that proceeds twilight. It's going to be full dark in no time. And here I am, taking a little boy into the woods.

It's too late to turn back now, so I put the car in park and button my coat to my chin. I reach into the backseat and fumble around for my knit hat, which I pull tight over my ears before daring to step out from the car. The drive took no more than ten minutes, probably less, yet I'm pretty sure the temperature dropped a degree each minute.

Maybe we should come back in the morning. Then again, I reason as I look around, no doubt we've already lost enough evidence out here. I don't want to risk losing more without at least getting a look at the place Benji described.

"Do me a favor?" I ask as Benji leads the way. In one gloved hand, I carry a flashlight, and when Benji isn't looking, I reach under my coat to pull my pistol free. I'll feel safer with it in my pocket, one hand wrapped around it. I don't know why, exactly, but a creepy chill that has nothing to do with the temperature skitters its way up my spine as we move deeper into the woods. I can't afford to creep myself out now, certainly, especially when there's a boy counting on me. Benji needs me to keep it together. So does Pete.

"What?" Benji asks, looking at me over his shoulder.

"For one thing, eyes forward. You don't want to twist an ankle because you weren't looking where you were going. What I was going to say is, I need you to promise not to come out here on your own. It doesn't matter the time of day or how well you know the area. I'd feel a lot better if you steer clear of the area for now, after tonight."

Like Pete, he's a good kid. The kind of kid who listens to authority without offering a ton of pushback. "Yeah, okay. Whatever you say."

"Thank you." What is it about this place that has me on edge? This isn't like me. I don't conjure ghosts where there are none. I don't get a thrill out of freaking myself out for no reason. The days of squealing and shrieking while hovering over a Ouija board are far in the past.

Yet I can't rid myself of a creeping sense of dread while following Benji to the river. For one brief, heart-stopping moment, I ask myself if this is all a ruse. A game. It wouldn't be the first time a kid killed someone who was supposed to be their friend, just to prove they could. What if he's playing me for a fool?

What if I'm acting like a fool with absolutely no prompting from him? I'm starting to think Mom and Dad, and Captain Felch and Mitch, and anyone else who's ever warned me against working too hard are right. Could it be I'm letting the job get to me too deeply? Every slight sound makes me jumpy, leaves me swinging the flashlight in a wide arc to get a look at the terrain around us. What do I think I'll find? The bogeyman?

In this case, that would mean Tyler Mahoney. I can't afford to obsess over him, and I can't do his dirty work by scaring myself to death. If he is out there,

Forest of Lies

pulling the strings, having fun watching me dance, I'll be darned if I let him poison me even when he's nowhere to be found.

"Watch your step." Benji holds his arms out to the sides before coming to a dead stop. "It's really steep here. And it's a little slippery."

I'm starting to think this was a bad idea. Yes, I'm beyond eager to find Pete and, I hope, help the captain and his family through this terrible situation. But I won't do much good if I wind up with a broken leg. I can practically see Mom's disappointed face in front of me, reacting to the news that her daughter took a stupid risk yet again.

Once we've navigated the slight dip in the terrain, I place a hand on Benji's shoulder to halt his progress. "Give me a second, please," I murmur, closing my hand tighter around the butt of the gun when the hair on the back of my neck rises. It's one thing to warn myself against letting my imagination run away with me. It's another to ignore my instincts. At the moment, they're screaming at me to be aware. On the lookout. For what, I don't know exactly. It's only that I've never felt so sure that I was being watched. This isn't my imagination. I feel it in my bones. Something is wrong here.

"Miss Forrest?" Benji's tentative question pulls me from my brain fog to find him wincing. "Sorry. Is there something else I should call you? Not officer, right?"

"Agent, but Alexis is fine." He's disarmingly respectful.

"Are you okay? We still have to go a little way." He gestures vaguely. "Are you tired? Maybe this wasn't a good idea?"

The disappointment rings heavy in his voice, strengthening my resolve. "No, I'm fine. It's only that I find myself wondering if I should have you out here in the cold and the dark."

"I can handle it." Only a fourteen-year-old, someone caught between childhood and adulthood, could manage to sound so confident and shaky at the same time. He wants to be brave. He wants to help his friend. I have to believe that's all there is to it. The kid isn't dangerous. Not everybody is a psycho waiting to strike.

It still does nothing to ease my tension as I look around again, searching for ... what? I don't honestly know anymore. The only thing I know is I would like this to be over as quickly as possible so I can go home where it's warm and comfortable and not so bleak and dangerous.

"Come on," I announce with a sigh, squaring my shoulders. "Let's keep going."

22

KILLER

That's right, little Alexis. You wander deeper into the dark, spooky woods. Ignore everything that trained mind of yours must be telling you. Keep going, keep trying to prove yourself.

I didn't expect to follow her anywhere beyond her little boyfriend's house this evening. As it turns out, she's still capable of surprising me. Isn't that what they say is the key to any long-lasting relationship? Our relationship has certainly lasted a long time, but she manages to keep me on my toes. I would congratulate her if I felt it was the right time to show myself. It isn't, but the time will come. And when it does, I'll go over this night with her. I'll describe in great detail the way I hung back far enough that she never noticed me tailing her to the woods. I'll describe my confusion and interest at the presence of a young boy. He's a curveball, a surprise guest star in the ongoing saga of our involvement. Well, variety is the spice of life.

Not for the first time am I glad I believe in preparation. One never knows what the day might bring, meaning I allow for as many scenarios as possible. I may not have predicted I'd take a hike today, but I always keep a good pair of boots and heavy gloves in the truck, just in case. Once I made certain Alexis wasn't going to double back to her car after climbing out, I shoved my feet into the boots and pulled on the gloves, then set out behind them.

It's slower going for me. I don't dare use a flashlight and announce my presence. I can't afford the glow from my phone, either. At first, I wonder if it might not be better to stay behind. I don't need to fall and break something. How would I get back to the truck?

Instead of taking the route Alexis does with the kid, I take the high road so to speak. The path sort of splits off, giving an explorer the choice between wandering close to the riverbank or staying further back, on higher ground. That's where I would want to be regardless. It gives me the chance to observe from above. Like God.

I wonder why he's taking her there. It isn't often I'm so curious, but then this is Alexis I'm talking about. Virtually everything about the way her mind works fascinates me. Her voice floats my way – I can't make out what she says, but I hear the pain she takes to sound commanding but also upbeat. Like they're nothing more than a pair of friends enjoying an evening stroll, even if the stroll involves bitter cold and increasing darkness.

Why are you here, little Alexis? The possibilities make my head spin. I'm almost giddy. What could she be on the hunt for? What is so important that it couldn't wait until morning? Then again, she doesn't strike me as the type to exercise patience once something catches her interest. In that respect, we are very much alike. There are times when the only thing holding me back from taking exactly what I want, when I want it, is the promise of the pleasure anticipation always brings. Years ago, I read a study whose results concluded humans take just as much pleasure in preparing for a big event as they do in the event itself. Anticipation is part of the fun, in other words. It increases happiness. I can testify to that myself. Many times, I've found myself happy that I was able to exercise patience and restraint. The results are always so much better when I do.

She's right there, though. So close, taking one step at a time while the kid leads her closer to the river. He's nothing. No one. History tells me it will be the easiest thing imaginable to cut him down. To end his young life, the way I've ended so many others. He wouldn't put up a fight, and if he did, it would take nothing to silence him.

I can see it in my head, crystal clear down to the last detail. The way Alexis would whirl on me. Her shock, her surprise. That moment when she would undoubtedly realize she had strayed too close to the spider's web. Not that I was waiting for her, not that I set this little trap. I didn't have to. The entire town of Broken Hill is my web.

She hasn't realized that yet, which is the problem. For her, not for me. My only problem is holding myself back rather than bursting from the trees and bringing to life every dark image now playing across my mind's eye like a movie. Something graphic, difficult to watch for so-called normal people who have never possessed the guts to admit their twisted, darkest thoughts. They're cowards, all of them. And somehow, they've managed to paint me as the bad guy. Pitiful. Projecting their complete lack of ambition and imagination onto me. Hating me for being who they only wish they could be.

The thought makes my blood pump and my mouth water. I'm hungry, so hungry, though it isn't food I'm interested in. She's so close. I could take her at any moment. No doubt her precious Mitch would spend hours pacing the floor, waiting for her call when it would never come. That gossiping mother of hers would once again know the pain of losing a child by my hand.

It would be so easy. There would be no one to stop me, no one even aware of what was happening. My entire body shakes hard enough to make my teeth chatter while I fight with myself. I need to do this. I can't resist. I won't rest tonight unless I indulge myself. Here. Now. They'll find the boy face down in the river tomorrow. He'll be a headline for a few days.

But Alexis? Alexis, I plan to keep with me. My pet, at least until she bores me. Then, I'll do what needs to be done. It's not something I look forward to, since I have come to appreciate her so much and to value the breath of fresh air she's brought me. Eventually, it would have to be done.

But not for a long, long time.

I lick my lips, fighting to control my breathing for fear of being heard before I'm ready to show myself. It always starts this way. The rush once I've made up my mind and given into my needs. I can hardly stay still, my body humming, adrenaline coursing through my veins.

Just a little further. I'll let them hike a little further, a little deeper, until I'm sure there's no chance of a scream being heard by anyone.

Anyone but me.

23

ALEXIS

"It's not much further! See? Up ahead."

I train the flashlight beam in the direction of Benji's extended arm and find what looks like an overhang close to the riverbank. "I see it."

I also see plenty of slippery rocks, a few of which are jagged in appearance. "Please, be careful," I urge. Do I sound like a frightened mother? It could be. I'm not Benji's mom, but I am responsible for him right now. I couldn't face his parents if I let anything happen to him.

"I've been down here lots of times. I know where to walk." I have to bite my tongue rather than remind him that's exactly how most accidents start. With someone feeling a little too cocky, too sure of themselves.

Forest of Lies

I'm on edge, that much is obvious. There is absolutely no shaking the prickling at the back of my neck. What's causing it? I snap my head around like that will do something to catch a predator unaware, and all I find behind me is the same darkness that exists in front of me. The only sound beyond that of my own breathing comes from the water flowing to my left. Water flowing loudly enough that if there were someone on our tail, we wouldn't be able to hear them until it was too late.

I'm being foolish. I'm sure the fact that we've been walking for much longer than I expected has something to do with it. There I was, thinking I would have Benji home in plenty of time for dinner, yet we've been walking for at least half an hour – and it feels like a lot more. My legs are numb by the time we reach the overhang and I stop to catch my breath.

"You okay?" Benji asks. "Don't, like, die on me. I'd be stuck out here."

His honesty is refreshing enough to make me laugh. "I won't leave you alone," I promise. "It's just the cold and dampness getting to me, I think."

He turns away from me, looking in all directions before he shivers. "It's kind of creepy at night. It doesn't feel that way during the day."

"That's when you have to remind yourself there's nothing in the darkness that doesn't exist in the light." That's a bunch of nonsense, but he's young enough to believe it. I knew better. There are plenty of things that can hide in darkness, that prefer darkness to cloak their activities. Monsters who wait all day for the sun to sink and the fun to begin.

No, it's certainly not the time to dwell on any of this. Rather than continuing to scare myself, I survey the area with the help of the flashlight beam. "Was there anything else that caught your eye when you first came out here?" I ask, noting the footprints I assume are Benji's. They fit the tread of his thick soled shoes, more like boots, warm and solid.

"Not really," he replies before removing his hat to scratch his head. His hair is matted down after hours spent covered up. "Not like anything unusual. I wish there was something more I could tell you."

"I know you do," I murmur. There's something so sincere about him. It's touching, but it also makes me a little sad. I can certainly relate to the frustration and helplessness of wanting to do well, to help someone while feeling completely useless.

Rather than dwell on that, I do what I can to keep him engaged while I study the area. "You guys come here a lot?" I ask.

"Not usually when it's this cold out."

A thought occurs to me and I look around again, this time trying to get a sense of where we are in terms of the rest of town. "How far is this from Pete's house? I'm a little turned around."

"A few minutes." He points across the river. "There's a little foot bridge around the bend. You can take that, climb up the bank, and you're practically on Pete's street. A couple of blocks and that's it."

"So it would be easy for him to come down here whenever he got the idea in his head."

"Yeah, but like I said, maybe when it's warmer out. That's why I was so surprised to find the book, too," he adds. "It's been so cold lately and snowing. And …"

He trails off. I watch him, noting the frown he can't hide in time. "And?" I prompt gently.

After blowing out a sigh that clouds in front of him, he continues, "And he used to spend a lot more time down here when his folks were together. Once, you know, things were getting bad and they were fighting a lot."

"It was an escape." I remember going through that sort of thing myself. "Sometimes, when your parents are fighting like cats and dogs, you just want to get away."

"Your parents do that?" He sounds incredulous.

"They're probably still doing it right now," I whisper, making him chuckle. "Yeah, I remember how that felt. When it gets really bad, you would do anything to get away from it."

"That's the kind of thing Pete would say."

"But you don't have to worry about that?"

Relief washes over his face before he shakes his head. "Nah. My parents gross me out. They're always kissing and stuff." He even gags a little, forcing me to stifle a laugh if I don't want to offend him.

"That's a lot better than hiding from fighting," I point out. He nods, and I'm sure an intelligent kid like him has already considered that. He seems very observant, but also introspective. In a way, he sort of reminds me of myself.

"Hold this for me?" I hand him the flashlight and demonstrate where I need him to train the beam. "I'm going to put up tape to mark the place for when I come back."

"You're coming back?" There's hope in the question, and it reminds me how touchingly young Benji is. He and Pete both. They're too young to see firsthand how ugly the world can be. What a shame there's no way of sheltering kids.

"In the morning, yes. It's much too dark now for me to get a firm grip on who might have been out here or when." Using the shrubbery around us, I set up a perimeter with the tape. My foot slips once, dangerously close to the river's edge, and a sick feeling slams into me before I can steady myself.

It's amazing how many possibilities can race through a person's mind all at once. I could see myself being laid up for weeks, if not much worse than that. What would that do to Benji, watching me fall into the river with no way of rescuing me? What if he went in after me, trying to help?

It's those questions that make up my mind. "We should go. It's high time I get you home. Give your mom a call and let her know we're heading back to the car now." Meanwhile, I take another look around, sliding my hand into my pocket, closing my fingers around the pistol once again. The sense of being watched is still there, as strong as ever.

I'm almost overtaken by the impulse to scream I know you're there. What good would it do? It would leave Benji thinking I'm out of my mind, and it might leave me inclined to agree with him.

The walk back to the car is even slower going thanks to the fatigue which has now caught up to both of us. This poor kid has been out all day. I should have offered to bring him out here tomorrow. He needs rest more than anything else, not to mention time spent in his warm home with his parents. He needs something normal after what has to be a terrible nightmare.

I could weep with joy once we reach the Corolla and practically throw ourselves inside. Many is the time I've lamented the car's heating system and how slow it is to wake up, but I don't think it's ever bothered me more than it does now. "Come on, already," I mutter, holding my hands over one vent while Benji does the same over the other. It's not long before warm air begins to flow through, thank goodness. Before long, we've thawed out enough for me to put the car in Drive and follow his directions home.

Now I remember more of what I learned about Pete's best friend. His father is an attorney, quite successful by the looks of the house Benji directs me too. "That's my mom and dad," he murmurs when the front door opens on our approach up the wide driveway. An attractive young couple appears on the front stoop, and Benji's mother waves as I pull to a stop.

"Better head in there. I'm sure they can't wait to hug you." Extending a hand, I add, "Thank you for being brave enough to go out looking for something that will help your friend."

He offers a bashful grin while accepting my handshake. "It's nothing. I just want him to come home."

Forest of Lies

Before he can pull away, I tighten my grip ever so slightly. "I'm going to need you to make me a promise."

Gee, what kind of hypocrite does this make me? How many times have I rolled my eyes inwardly – if not outwardly – when approached in a similar fashion? "I need you to promise you're not going to go back out there by yourself. Especially when the water is as high as it is now. One missing person is enough. Hear what I'm saying?"

His lips pull into a tight line, but he nods slowly. "Yeah. I hear you."

"Okay. I'll let you know whenever we hear anything, and you can give me a call at the station if there's anything you think of that might be helpful." He promises to do that, then exits the car. Even with the windows rolled up, I can hear his mother peppering him with questions before finally giving up and throwing her arms around him. For some reason, the sight fills me with melancholy.

Maybe because I can't help but think of Becky and how much she would give to throw her arms around her little boy.

The thought tightens my jaw as I pull away. Rather than head home or to Mitch's, I point the car in the direction of the station. I want to confirm Pete's book is entered into evidence, then do a little more digging through the notes the deputies compiled during their interviews. There has to be something we've missed.

24

ALEXIS

If it weren't so cold out, I might consider sleeping in the car. Right now, as exhausted as I am, the idea of walking up the front steps of Mitch's house is too much to handle. After that, it will mean climbing even more stairs before crawling into bed.

It's nobody's fault but my own. Once I got started diving deeper into Pete's case, the hours flew by. I admit, I haven't given the case as much attention as it might need, mostly thanks to personal worries. I did tell the captain I would help in any way I could, and so far I haven't done much to make good on that.

By the time words started blurring in front of my eyes, it was nearing eleven o'clock. Now here I am, dragging myself up to the house, looking both ways in case somebody decided to pay a visit tonight. The street is as empty and quiet as I would expect at this hour.

For some reason that doesn't offer much comfort. Mostly because it seemed quiet out here the night, Mitch's tires were slashed. Appearances are deceiving.

The interior of the house is dark and quiet, and right away I face a wave of regret. Aside from a quick message letting Mitch know I wouldn't be leaving the station as early as I had planned, I left him hanging tonight. I'll have to find a way to make it up to him. The best thing I can do right now is move as quietly as possible, tiptoeing up the stairs, holding my breath as I creep down the hall. The bedroom door is ajar but there's no light on inside. Waking up as early as he does, I'm sure he's been in bed for at least an hour. It's nice to know he's here, knowing there's someone to curl up next to at the end of a long, frustrating day.

He is a softly snoring lump under the covers by the time I creep into the room. Right away, I take off my shoes, leaving them beside the door so I can move soundlessly toward the dresser. I'm familiar enough with the room that I can get around without too much trouble, and besides, he's a sound sleeper.

Once I'm in my pajamas, I tiptoe to the bed. I wonder if he'll be surprised when he wakes up and finds me here. He must've expected me, since he left the door unlocked. Strange that he wouldn't text to let me know. Maybe he figured I was too busy to read it.

I've just about accomplished my goal of sneaking in when, swinging my leg into bed, I catch my toe against the edge of the bedframe hard enough to make me suck in a pained gasp through my clenched teeth. It's just loud enough to make Mitch stir, then roll over to face me.

"Sorry," I whisper in the dark. "I'm fine. You can go back to sleep."

He releases a sleepy grunt. "What time is it?"

"A little after eleven. No, it was after eleven when I left the station," I murmur, "so I guess it's probably half-past or so? I totally lost track of time, and what's worse, I didn't really make any headway."

I'm babbling, I realize. "Sorry. Really, go back to sleep. We can talk about it tomorrow."

"No, please. Tell me more. What did you do tonight?"

I'm so glad he asked, as it turns out. What I want more than a good night's sleep is the opportunity to talk about the way the night unfolded. "I was just about to leave when Pete's best friend showed up at the station. A nice kid, he seems sweet and worried." It all pours out of me—the trip to the woods, the walk along the river, my intention to return in the morning.

"So let me get this straight." By the time I'm finished, Mitch sounds a lot more awake than he did before. He props himself up on one elbow, and now that my eyes have fully adjusted to the darkness, I see the way he stares at me. "You took that kid down to the river past dark, when nobody knew where you were. Then, instead of coming here afterward, you went back to the station without giving anybody the heads up as to what your plans were. Including and especially the person who was waiting here for you. You didn't bother texting me until well past eight to tell me you were still at the station. Beyond that, you didn't think to keep me in the loop at all."

My head is spinning. Which one of his points do I address first? Is there any point in defending myself? "I'm sorry," I manage to sputter. "I really am. It's just—"

"No, I don't want to hear what it's just." He pushes himself up into a sitting position all at once, swinging his legs over the bed so I'm staring at his back. "Just when I think we're in a good place where we understand each other, you have to remind me that I will always come second to work. Everything else in your life falls by the wayside when it comes to work."

"That isn't true."

"I think it is." When I reach out to him, barely brushing my fingertips against his t-shirt, he jumps to his feet like my touch burns. "And what were you thinking, taking a kid out like that? It's one thing for you to take unnecessary risks, but to involve a fourteen-year-old kid? When you know there's somebody out there who could be watching you, somebody with a grudge against you? What were you thinking?"

I wasn't. That's the problem. "I wanted to have him show me where he found the book before any more damage was done to the scene."

"What damage? What scene? I don't pretend to know everything about what it is you do," Mitch mumbles, scrubbing his hands over his head. The sight of his slumped shoulders, the way he sighs, none of it fills me with positive feelings. "But I do know you can't turn every little thing into an emergency. It could have waited. At the very least, you might have kept me posted throughout the night so I wouldn't have to sit here worrying about you. It wouldn't be the first time you decided to run out at a moment's notice to chase some dangerous lead by yourself."

My desperate, flailing mind grabs onto that with all the tenacity of a bulldog. "You sure looked like you were worrying when I came in." I fold my arms, giving him the same steely look he's giving me. "You were dead asleep."

"Because eventually, I had to remember the fact that I have my own business to run and my own employees to consider, and I needed to get to sleep."

"All I'm saying is, don't turn this into more than it is. That's all."

"You refuse to get it." He sounds dejected. I wish I weren't so angry. Otherwise, I would want to comfort him. "This isn't normal. This is not what I want."

Silence unfurls, bringing the temperature down until I'm surprised my breath doesn't fog in the air. "What are you saying?" I whisper with my heart in my throat. What is happening here? How did things devolve like this?

After sputtering a few moments, he throws his hands into the air. "I don't know. I don't know what I'm saying. But I know how I'm feeling, And what I'm feeling is missing a time when I could have a normal relationship with a normal girlfriend I wasn't constantly worried about."

"You keep using that word."

"Because that's how it is. Stop being dense about this. You put yourself into situations where you could get hurt, and you do it constantly. Do you know what it's like caring about somebody who is constantly putting themselves in harm's way?"

"I don't know what you want me to say," I admit. At first, it's all I can get out thanks to the way my throat has tightened. My heart is pounding thanks to the sense of being attacked. Judged. He won't even let me defend myself.

"There's nothing to be said. Maybe it's time for you to listen instead of speaking."

"I need to listen?" See, that's a little too much for me to swallow. I can accept his disappointment and even irritation, but accusing me of not listening? "Maybe you are the one with the problem listening and understanding. Do you know what it's like having somebody come to you and ask you to find a loved one? When someone is counting on you? And there's nothing you can do right away to bring that person back. All you can do is fight for every clue. Chase down every lead. Even if it seems ridiculous, even if it might be a waste of time, and even if it's dangerous. I understand your frustration, and I wish things were different. I really do. But I am not going to apologize for having this responsibility on my shoulders. Sometimes, my work means putting myself in harm's way."

"Do you have to go around actively searching for danger?"

"I never do!" By now we're both at full volume and getting louder. The small part of my brain still capable of rational thought hates it. I know this is wrong, that we need to end the argument before either of us says something we can't take back.

With a weary sigh, he sinks to the bed again, facing away from me. All I can do is watch the rise and fall of his shoulders, wishing I could make him understand. I know I'm not perfect. I can be forgetful when I'm in the middle of something time sensitive or important. It isn't that I want to hurt anybody. How can I make him see?

"This is getting us nowhere." Just as quickly as he got up, Mitch settles back into bed and pulls the blankets up to his shoulders, facing away from me. "We can talk about it tomorrow."

He's not wrong. All we're doing now is talking at each other, not to each other. We could only make things worse by digging our heels in and demanding the other one see our point of view.

It's better to wait, even if that means lying in the dark, staring at the ceiling, waiting in vain for him to start snoring. Then, I would know he fell asleep. Minutes pass, too many of them, and still there's nothing but silence.

Maybe I'd better get used to that silence. Maybe I had better practice the feeling of being alone,

Forest of Lies

isolated, because I am not sure I'm cut out for this whole relationship thing. If I can't make it work with Mitch – the most supportive, understanding man to ever breathe air – how can I hope to make it work with anyone?

Besides, I don't want anyone else. I want Mitch, but all I seem to do is disappoint him and worry him.

How can we last this way?

Have I been kidding myself all this time? Telling myself I can do what so many people in my shoes were never able to pull off. Telling myself I'm different, that I can strike a balance between work and my personal life.

Have I been lying to myself?

25

ALEXIS

I can't believe I'm glad Mitch is already gone for the morning by the time I wake up. If there is one thing I would never have believed, it's that there would ever come a time when I would rather not see him first thing in the morning.

When I open my eyes to find faint, gray light filling the room, my gaze immediately falls upon his empty pillow. The bathroom door is open, the light off. I grab for my phone, sitting on the nightstand, and find it's well past six. He's been gone for a while. Probably right around the time I finally fell asleep for real. Come to think of it, since that's usually when I sleep the deepest, in the first couple of hours. Before that, there were a few hours of thin, restless dozing filled with ugly, half-realized dreams that kept stirring me out of my pitiful slumber.

Forest of Lies

Nightmares of being left alone. Losing what could be the best thing that's ever happened to me.

I'm hoping like crazy things have cooled down. I'm hoping Mitch was feeling extra reactionary last night, and he's now feeling calmer after having slept. At least, I hope he slept.

I'm achy after having spent hours tossing and turning. Throwing my arms over my head, I stretch and groan and try to shake off the fog. I was already planning on going back to the river today to examine the area more carefully. Now, I have to fix things with Mitch, too. I'm not sure how I'm going to make it happen, but there has to be a way.

One thing becomes abundantly clear once I've gotten out of bed, I need more clothes. There was a limited supply here in the first place, and what's left at the moment isn't suitable for work. If anything, I'm glad for an excuse to stop in at Mom's. If I show up with a reason for being there, they might not be suspicious of my motives. I doubt either of them would enjoy hearing I've been worried they would find a way to kill each other, being alone together for the first time in years.

Stepping outside after bundling up and double checking the locks, I groan to myself. I'm not exactly surprised at the biting cold that immediately leaks through my coat and scarf to chill my skin. It doesn't bode well for my trip to the river, unfortunately. Once I'm in the car, I check the weather app on my phone and find the temperature won't come anywhere close to the freezing mark.

My discomfort doesn't matter. Pete is still out there somewhere, and his mother must be beyond overwrought by now. My jaw is set in grim determination throughout the ride to Mom's. It would be easy to lose myself in worry over Mitch, but I can't let that happen. Pete needs my focus.

If only I could make Mitch understand that. I tried last night, but he was not in the mood to hear it. And the thing is, I know he understands. But everyone has a breaking point. It just so happens I have a talent for helping people find them.

Everything looks peaceful and normal at the house when I park close to the driveway. No broken windows, no possessions strewn over the front lawn. Not that I truly believe things would ever get to that point, but I've also learned not to discount what seems impossible. People generally find a way to surprise even those who know them and love them best. I mean, I would never have imagined my father attempting murder ... until he did.

Not that I think he would ever try anything like that with Mom. I shake my head at myself, snickering at the dark, overly dramatic direction my thoughts have taken. I need more than a good night's sleep. I think I might need a vacation.

I'm careful to be quiet upon entering the house. I don't doubt Mom would be awake by now, but I don't know about Dad's sleeping habits. If he's still in bed in the guestroom, I can sneak in and out without bothering him. I know exactly what I need and where to find it.

Avoiding a creaky floorboard, I take hold of the door knob and turn it slowly, holding my breath before I ease the door open. The bed is empty. After poking my head into the room, I see the bathroom door standing open. That room, too, is empty. He's already up, though, I don't hear him anywhere around the house.

Oh, what if he decided to leave? I don't know who I'm more disappointed in if that turns out to be the case. I'm distracted, worried as I gather a handful of items, then change into a fresh outfit before venturing out of the room again with a few pieces of clothing tucked under my arm. Just in case I make things right with Mitch.

The kitchen seems like the most likely place to find Mom, so I head down the hall, ready to either scold her for driving Dad away or sympathize with her because he is very stubborn when he puts his mind to it. It could just as easily be a matter of him refusing to peacefully coexist after years spent alone. I'm sure it's not easy on him, being back here.

By the time I round the kitchen doorway, I'm prepared for anything. Or so I tell myself.

Nothing could have prepared me for what I find. It's not so much how close they're standing to each other, but the way they're looking at each other while they do it. The hand Dad touches to the small of Mom's back, rubbing it in slow circles while she scrambles eggs on the stove. That tiny gesture hits me like the shockwave from an atomic blast. I've witnessed this same moment more times than I can possibly count, the casual intimacy, the sense of the two of them being the only two people in the world.

Only it's been twenty years since the last time I've seen it.

"What is happening?" I ask, watching as they both jump, startled.

It's a one-two punch. First, the casual intimacy. Now, the guilt. The way Dad instantly backs off, putting space between them. Like a couple of teenagers caught fooling around when they thought all of the grown-ups were in bed for the night.

"Honey." Mom pats her hair before running a hand over the front of her buttoned cardigan. "When did you show up? You're like a ghost!" Her laughter is suspiciously high-pitched, full of nerves.

"I needed clothes." And I'm in no mood to be distracted. Turning from her toward Dad, I raise my eyebrows. "What did I walk in on? Is there something you haven't told me?"

"Alexis…" Dad offers a weak shrug. "I don't know what you want us to say."

"Oh, duh!" I slap a palm to my forehead, then wave back-and-forth between them. "You didn't even sleep in the guestroom, did you? That bed was untouched since I last saw it. I can't believe this!"

"Would you please calm down?" Mom folds her arms after moving the pan off the hot burner. "I fail to see how any of this involves you."

"Oh, very nice," I retort. "No, I guess it would be too much for you to ask how this would look to me. For years, I've gone back and forth between the two of you. Trying to keep the peace. Worrying about you both. Feeling like I couldn't be too close to one of you, because it would be unfaithful to the other. All it took was a few hours back together, and all of that is forgotten?"

"You are making too much out of this." Dad slides his hands into the pockets of his jeans, scowling. "By now, you know your mother and I are grown adults with a history of our own. This is our situation to navigate."

And what about me? I hear the question ringing in my head, and even now, confused and frustrated, I know it wouldn't be right to say it out loud. I would be embarrassed to voice something that childish.

Instead, I do something equally as childish. "You know what? Forget it. Have fun together. Just don't expect me to be around to pick up the pieces with you when things fall apart." I can't bear to look at them anymore, turning on my heel and ignoring them when they call out behind me on my march to the front door. I don't want to hear anything they have to say right now.

I am thirty years old. I should be way beyond this immature, resentful behavior. It's almost like I'm watching myself from outside my body as I slam my way into the car and peel away from the curb faster than I would normally drive.

What about me? So many times, they've made decisions without considering me. When Dad fired on Russell Duffy outside the courthouse and tore our already frayed lives to shreds. When Mom decided to settle down with another man who could not have been worse for her if she had set out looking for the worst possible partner.

But I'm only halfway to the station before good sense begins to filter through the angry cloud that's built up around me. Is this the person I want to be? Instead of being glad my parents seem to be reconciling, I blew up at them. They are two people who could use a little comfort, but I chose to resent them for it.

And Mitch. I've watched my parents make mistakes, pushing each other away, allowing themselves to get lost in their pain and lose sight of each other. Yet here I am, making a similar mistake with Mitch. Losing sight of what matters more than anything. Having someone to come home to, a constant. Because in the end, work is not enough. Once the case is solved, what is there? Sure, there will always be another case, but what about everything else that matters?

I don't like the person I'm becoming. Somebody who would begrudge the happiness of people I love. Why was that not the first thing I thought of when I saw them together? Sure, it was a surprise, but I took it personally. I took it too hard, even when it really has nothing to do with me. I'm not a kid anymore. I have a life of my own. Why act like their decisions play such an important role in my life?

I'm no closer to answers by the time I reach the police station. Part of me wants to turn the car around and go back to Mom's, to apologize for acting like a brat, but the clock is still ticking on Pete McClintock. I'll have to touch base with them later, and hopefully by then I'll be able to put my thoughts into words that aren't childish or spiteful.

All I know for sure as I hustle into the station, avoiding the biting cold, is that I'm batting a thousand when it comes to my personal life. I hope today brings a professional win, or else I might have to scream.

26

ALEXIS

"Agent Forrest?"

It's not until I hear the raised voice of one of the officers studying the scene that I realize my thoughts wandered. Again. He's looking at me like he's concerned. Or like I've grown a second head.

I jam my hands into my pockets—the presence of gloves doesn't seem to matter, since they're half-numb after a couple of hours spent out here. "I'm sorry. What was it you were trying to say?" I ask.

There is an uncomfortable moment where he stares at me like I'm losing my mind. "I was asking you to step aside so I can move past."

And now I want to wither on the spot. "Sorry." I press myself close to the rock face only a few feet from the overhang where Pete's book was found.

Things are pretty crowded around here thanks to the five officers, plus me.

This is the last place I want to be right now. I can hardly believe myself—last night, after leaving, I couldn't wait to get back once there was enough light to see. It was all that mattered. Incredible how our priorities can change. It isn't that Pete is no longer important. It's that there are trained officers here on the scene who know what to look for. I could and maybe should be working on other things.

It's absolutely miserable out here, and not only because I would rather be with Mitch. Every minute spent out in the bitter cold, treading wet ground while ducking countless twigs and branches is a minute I could be trying to make things better for us. I'm no good out here, anyway. I may as well be walking in my sleep, going through the motions but not paying attention to much of anything.

Is this what it means to worry about filling my own cup before I can pour water into somebody else's? I've always heard that saying, and it makes sense—even if I've never been able to put it to use in my own life. I'm starting to see how it's applicable here. How I can't be any help to Pete unless I take care of myself first. I am exhausted, heartsick, disappointed in myself. I'm sad, so sad it's distracting. I'm not helping anybody like this.

I'm stuck in an endless loop of insanity, repeating the same actions and expecting a different solution. It's time to slam on the brakes.

"Agent Forrest? Where are you going?" The officers exchange confused looks. It was my big idea to come out here in the first place, after all. I can understand their concern when I suddenly begin walking away.

"I just remembered something else I need to attend to. But I have every bit of faith in you," I assure them. "You can reach me on my cell if you find anything new."

For the first time all day, I feel like I'm making the right choice. Heading back to the car, moving a lot quicker than I was able to last night. What was a long walk in the dark is much shorter now, and it helps that I'm in something of a hurry. That's what happens once you make up your mind sometimes, I guess. Suddenly, there's somewhere you absolutely need to be, forget the consequences.

I don't know what I need to say to Mitch to make things better, but I have to try. I don't care what it takes short of quitting my job, which I know he would never ask me to do. Otherwise, I'm willing to agree to just about anything. Nothing matters as much as him. Us. Somehow, there must be a way I can stop losing sight of that. A way for me to put us first, always, the way it ought to be.

My heart's ready to burst by the time I pull onto Main Street, and the little bit of traffic standing in my way leaves me wanting to tap the horn. I'm that eager to get to him.

By the time I find a parking spot, the clouds have broken and the sun is shining. I'm going to choose to take that as a good sign, like Mother Nature herself is cheering me on as I jog down the street, caught between feeling like the heroine out of a romantic comedy and a complete idiot who can probably be recognized by people passing in their cars. Let them recognize me. For the first time in days, I'm doing exactly what I need to do, exactly when I need to do it.

The store is as busy as I would expect it to be on a Sunday morning, with customers wandering among the rows of bookshelves. A few of them sit together in front of the fireplace with books open on their laps, engaged in deep conversation while others take their purchases back to the café so they can read while sipping coffee. It's a warm, inviting atmosphere. How nice would it be if my work gave me experiences like this? Instead of constantly running down leads, I could go on and on about my favorite books while eating muffins and sipping lattes.

Mitch is in the middle of clearing a table when he notices me marching his way. He is as heartbreakingly handsome as ever, his blue eyes standing out brighter than usual thanks to his cream colored cable knit. "Alexis. What —"

Before he can say another word, I remove the pair of plates he's holding and return them to the table. I then take his face in my hands and pull him down while standing on tiptoe for a hard, deep kiss that darn near makes my hair stand on end and earns gentle applause from the customers around us. By the time I let him up for air, Mitch's arms are around my waist – gentle, though almost tentative.

"What was that all about?" He sounds dazed, though there's a touch of laughter in his voice.

"That was to tell you I'm sorry. I'm a total idiot. I keep making the same mistakes over and over, and I am so lucky you even want to be around to call me on it. I want you to stay around. I need you. And if it takes marching into your store and kissing you in front of everybody, that's what I'll do. Because I couldn't wait another minute to tell you how sorry I am for ever hurting or worrying you. You deserve better than that." By the time I'm finished, I need to take a deep breath. It all poured out of me at once. I can only hope it's enough.

The faint lines at the corners of his eyes deepen when he smiles. "Okay, okay." He tightens his grip on me, pulling me closer, and my heart might burst if this keeps up. "You're forgiven. I'm afraid if I don't forgive you, you'll kiss me again like you just did, and things might get a little awkward." He clears his throat and winces, making me giggle before he leans down to deliver a much softer, safer kiss that still gets the point across. We are all right. We can get through this.

"Thank you," I whisper. "Thank you, thank you for giving me another chance."

"Well, I could've handled things better, too." I'm about to take all of the responsibility for this on myself when he shakes his head. "I could have called you at the station to check in, but I told myself I should wait to see if you would call. The longer I waited, the more determined I was to keep waiting. I guess I wanted to be able to hold it over your head. I still don't think it's okay that you take risks without thinking it through, and I do wish you would work on that, but it's only because I don't want to go back to life without you."

"I promise, I'm going to do my best from now on. I'll keep you in mind. I swear."

"I guess that will have to do. If I can't get you to be careful for your own sake, then you'll need to be careful for mine." He presses a kiss against the tip of my nose before looking around. "All right. We still have an audience. Let me clear this table and get back to work before the town starts getting ideas about what goes on in here during business hours."

Forest of Lies

I don't have the heart to tell him half the town will probably already hear about this by the time dinner rolls around. That's how things tend to go in Broken Hill. Then again, he knows that as well as I do.

I help him without thinking, clearing a pair of mugs from the table. "I have an idea. Why don't we go away for a few days? Can you swing it?"

His eyes light up when they meet mine. "I would love to. When were you thinking?"

"As soon as possible."

His head snaps back, and he pauses halfway through wiping the table down. "Oh, that soon? What's the hurry?"

"I think we could use it, and I know I could. I have to get away for a little bit. I need to reset my head." I doubt I've ever needed it more, considering the tantrum I threw this morning. I still can't get it out of my head, nor can I stop cringing every time I think about it.

"Well … " He strokes his jaw, his gaze going on unfocused as he thinks it over. "I could do that. Earlier in the week is normally the slowest time around here, and I can juggle the schedule a little to make sure I'm fully covered."

"Good. That settles it. I'll take care of everything, you don't have to do anything but pack your clothes."

"Are you going to clue me in as to where we're going?" he asks with a laugh.

"I don't know. I was thinking … maybe Martha's Vineyard?" I suggest, shrugging. "It's the off-season, and there's bound to be rooms available during the week even at the last minute."

His easy grin is exactly what I needed to see. "That sounds great to me. I am entirely in your hands."

And for the first time all day, it feels like life is back on track.

27

ALEXIS

"I hope you understand that I really need to take a few nights away. I'm not doing you or anybody else any good by burning myself out. I realize this is probably the worst possible time to decide to take a short vacation, but it's pretty clear I'll either do this or tank my whole life."

I have to laugh at myself as I look out the front window of Mitch's living room. He's waiting for me in his truck, our bags already loaded in. From the looks of it, he's fiddling with his playlist. "You don't need to hear about my personal issues," I continue with a sigh, babbling away on Captain Felch's voicemail. I was hoping he would be around to answer his phone, but it seems he hasn't checked in at the station yet this morning.

I'm a little concerned about him, but there's no predicting how a person will behave when they are in the middle of the sort of nightmare his family is still living with. "I checked in with the officers who went over the scene at the river. There was nothing else there to give any indication of Pete's presence. It could be the book happened to be left behind, that he might have forgotten it. The book is still being processed for prints or any other evidence."

I feel like I should offer something else. "Please, let me know if anything else comes up. I'll have my phone on all the time." With that, I end the call probably much later than I should have. I hate leaving voicemails sometimes. It's so easy to lose track of what I've already said and what I mean to say.

I'm never going to get over feeling like I'm letting him down by going away at such a bad time for him. Sadly, facts are facts. It seems more and more all the time like Pete vanished without a trace. I know there's no such thing, and I know there's less of a chance every day of this having a happy ending.

At the same time, the calls I made to both Mom and Dad went unanswered and unreturned. I'm lucky I managed to make up with Mitch, and I know eventually I'll make up with them as well. If I weren't run ragged, I might not have made such childish mistakes in the first place. I need to know when it's time to take a step back. If all the drama I managed to create in my life is any indication, there has never been a better time for me to pop away for a few days.

After double checking to make sure the house is locked up, I waste no time heading out to the truck. "Come on!" Mitch urges. "We have a vacation to take." From the sound of it, he needs this as much as I do.

Once we pull away from the curb, it's real. I can release a deep breath and let myself melt against the seat. "Is it possible for me to already feel better?" I ask as the sounds of classic rock fill the truck. It's a bright, sunny day, and we have nothing on the agenda besides being together. In other words, I'm on top of the world.

Mitch's hand closes over my knee as he turns down Main Street. "I'm glad you feel better. Keep it up. Let yourself relax."

"This is about you, too," I remind him.

"I'll relax once the driving is over," he jokes. I know better than to offer to take over for him. He prefers to be the one behind the wheel. Besides, I sort of like the idea of being the passenger, sitting back and letting him handle things. It lets me admire the scenery.

It's around a four hour drive, which gives us plenty of time to talk about everything and nothing at the same time. "You know," I muse, staring out the window to my right and watching the sun paint the bare trees in the distance, "being down at the river reminded me of a few of the parties we threw down there. Remember?"

"I'm not sure how much I could possibly remember, seeing as how all we tried to do was get as messed up as we could, as quickly as we could," Mitch admits. We share a knowing laugh, the kind of laughter that only comes from a lifetime of experience. There's nothing quite like looking back at how stupid you were when you were a kid.

"I'm amazed none of us broke our necks or ended up drowning," I confess. "It's wild to look back and ask myself what the heck I was thinking."

"I know. Clearly, we all had guardian angels looking after us." He looks my way wearing a funny little smile. "Could you have imagined yourself sitting here next to me all these years later? Be honest."

"Ouch." I squirm a little in my seat, pretending to be uncomfortable. "You know how to put a girl on the spot, don't you?"

"Consider it repayment for all the grief you've put me through lately."

"I thought this trip was repayment," I counter. All he does is growl, so I have to relent. "Fine, fine. Could I see myself here, now? No, but not because it wasn't what I wanted. It was – we were."

"But?"

"But ... I mean, let's face it. I didn't exactly have the best possible example of a forever kind of love, you know what I mean? Dad was in prison, Mom was doing everything she could to deal with that, and with losing Maddie, and with raising me on her own. I wasn't looking toward a happy future – as depressing as that sounds."

"I didn't mean to bring the mood down," he offers in a quiet voice.

"I know. And you didn't. It's just ... I never really thought about it before, I guess. I think what I wanted more than anything back then was to get out of here. Not to get away from you. To get away from everything else."

"Of course. And nobody could blame you for that."

"What about you?" I tease, nudging him. "Did you see us like this one day?"

"Oh, absolutely."

How does he do it? How does he take my breath away with two simple words? It's the way he didn't have to think about it. The utter certainty in his voice. Once I've caught my breath, I offer, "I'm sorry I kept you waiting."

"Some people are worth waiting for." Just when I'm about to swoon, he adds, "I mean, don't get me wrong. It's not like I lived the life of a monk all the time you were gone."

"Oh? Are we going to get on this topic now? Because I would like to hear about your life while I was away." I angle my body so I'm facing him, hands folded in my lap. "So. Tell me all about it."

It's his turn to squirm. "Now I'm starting to wish I had never said anything."

"You mean you don't want to regale me with tales of all the women whose hearts you've broken over the years?"

"I wouldn't go that far." He glances my way and shakes his head. "That's the most you're going to get out of me. A gentleman doesn't kiss and tell."

"Fine. You're off the hook." I don't really want to hear about it, anyway. Who would?

"I wonder how things are going over at your mom's," he murmurs.

I swing back around in my seat, facing forward again. "Well. There's a way to change the subject."

I love the sound of his laughter. "I'm serious, though," he insists before laughing again. "I wonder how it's going."

"For all I know, they're planning their second wedding."

Forest of Lies

"There's nothing wrong with a couple of people who share history reaching out to each other and reconnecting. Isn't that what we've done?"

"Sure, but they're divorced."

"That had nothing to do with their feelings for each other – no," he amends, shaking his head. "I take that back. It absolutely did. Your dad wanted a divorce so your mom would be free. He knew he made a mistake. He didn't want her to have to pay for it for the rest of her life. Now, that might not have been the best choice, but it was what he felt like he had to do. That doesn't mean the feelings went anywhere."

He's so right. Now I feel worse than ever about giving them such a hard time. "Do you think it will be possible for you to accompany me everywhere I go, all the time, forever? Because you are much better at handling just about everything than I am."

"Don't sell yourself short. There's plenty of things you're better at than me."

"Like what?"

"Getting into trouble."

"You know, I could call and cancel this reservation in no time." Not that I would. The further we get from Broken Hill, the better I feel. The easier it is to breathe. To think. To remember that I am an actual

229

person with an actual life, and I deserve a little time for myself. It's very easy to lose sight of that when I'm constantly neck deep in a case.

We're somewhere outside Boston when Mitch asks a question that makes my heart skip a beat. "Where do you see yourself in five years?"

Why does this feel like a much bigger question than it appears on the surface? Suddenly, my palms are clammy and my tongue feels too thick. I don't want to say the wrong thing. Not when we're doing so well right now and feeling so happy. "The truth?"

"I wouldn't have asked if I didn't want the truth."

"To be honest, I never really thought about it. I figured I would just ... work. That's what I do. I work, and the rest of my life sort of fills in the gaps around that. Or it used to."

"But not anymore?"

Rubbing his arm, I murmur, "No, things have definitely changed."

"For the better?"

"Yes, very much for the better."

There's a few moments of pleasant silence before he offers, "For what it's worth, I would never tell you to stop working. I want you to have your career. I know how important it is to you, and I know how much fulfillment you get out of it. All I ask is that you take a little time for the rest of your life. The way you are right now. So long as you don't forget about us."

"I promise. I'm going to do everything I can to put us front and center. You have my word on it. But, you know, feel free to tell me to get over myself whenever I start losing sight of what matters."

"It's a deal." Just when I imagine this topic has come to a close, he asks one more question. "Have you ever thought about marriage?"

Whoa. This got very heavy, very fast. Not in a bad way. More in a deer in headlights sort of way. It's a good thing I'm not eating, or I might have choked on my surprise. "Are you talking in general or specifically?"

"Just in general," he assures me in his usual laid-back way. "Have you ever imagined yourself getting married?"

Boy, oh boy. Does he know how to shake me up. He deserves an honest response, so I give the question real thought. "To tell you the truth, not as an adult. When I was a kid, sure, but as I've gotten older, the idea faded. But I'm sure that had something to do with the lack of men worth marrying. Not every man is as perfect as you."

"Have you thought about it with me?"

I walked right into that one, didn't I? Here's hoping he likes the only truthful answer I can give him. "I'm a big fan of living together before taking that step. I think jumping straight into marriage might be a little too much, too fast. Too many people jump into it without really understanding what it takes or even who it is they've decided to commit their life to. Know what I mean?"

"You're right. It does make more sense to live together first." From the corner of my eye, I catch him grinning, and that grin lasts a long time. I can feel his relief, and I know I gave him the right answer. What a good thing it happened to be the truth.

This trip is looking like a better idea all the time.

28

ALEXIS

Dropping his napkin onto his plate, Mitch leans back in his chair with a happy sigh. "I'm afraid you're going to have to roll me down the street," he groans, patting his belly. "I'm afraid I made a pig out of myself."

It's easy to do when the food is so delicious. "Maybe it's the change in locale or the sea air," I suggest after looking down at what little is left of my patty melt and fries. "I'm going to need a long, long walk to work this off."

As soon as he arches an eyebrow, I know the direction his thoughts have led him. "I can think of other ways to work it off," he points out in a suggestive tone.

"And here you were just seconds ago, telling me I would have to roll you down the street. You sure know how to rally when you feel like it."

"Take it as a compliment." He lifts a shoulder while I try to stifle a laugh. Not that I mind being wanted. Far from it. And it isn't like I came to the Vineyard unprepared — there are a few special pieces of underwear in my luggage. Certain things are implied by a quick getaway with one's boyfriend.

"Do you think you have the stamina for a nice walk on the beach before we get down to any of that sort of thing?" Yes, it's cold, but the air doesn't have the same bitter, biting quality. It could be my imagination, of course – it's easy to go on a trip and imagine everything being a little different than it is back home. All I know is, the walk here from the bed-and-breakfast was pleasant enough that I was able to unbutton my coat. After spending all this time freezing on a daily basis, it feels downright balmy by comparison.

Once we're outside, Mitch takes my hand before we begin to walk. "Have you spent a lot of time here?" he asks. Our pace is leisurely, which is fine by me. That's another thing about being away. There's no hurry. It's enough to be together.

"I came through once, years ago, but it was the busy season. You could barely elbow your way down the sidewalk." That is not the case now, with only a handful of pedestrians passing us as we walk through the quaint village. In many ways it reminds me of Broken Hill, where tourist dollars are key to keeping the town going. Being here as a tourist rather than a resident is refreshing. This is the peace and quiet my soul craved, and I couldn't be more grateful.

I couldn't be more grateful for Mitch, either, and my heart skips a beat when he catches me looking at him. "What's up?" he asks with a playful grin.

"Nothing. For the first time in weeks, absolutely nothing. And I couldn't be happier about that." He drops my hand in favor of wrapping an arm around me, and I lean against him with a grateful smile.

As it turns out, a walk along the beach is what I needed to get rid of the heavy feeling left over after stuffing myself. There is nothing like sea air, that's for sure. I make it a point to take big, deep breaths, hoping to soak in as much of it as I can. I need to bring this feeling home with me.

By the time we return to the bed and breakfast, where we left our bags earlier, we're both windblown and almost giddy with relief thanks to the fire crackling merrily in our room. The word charming doesn't do it justice, with a four poster brass bed covered in what looks like a handmade quilt, a pair of rocking chairs in front of the fire, even a stained glass window that sends beams of red, blue, and green light throughout the room thanks to the sun streaming through it.

Right away, I hustle over to the fireplace and hold my hands close to the grate. "That cold sneaks up on you," I laugh, rubbing them together before holding them out again.

A pair of arms slide around me from behind, and soon there's warm breath against the back of my neck. "I can think of even better ways to warm up," Mitch murmurs before touching his lips to my skin.

Who am I to say no to that?

"Hey, look here."

I am busy admiring the idyllic shops across the street from where we walk to dinner, but now Mitch has pulled me to a stop. Confused, I follow the direction his attention has taken—and then root myself to the sidewalk when he gives my hand a tug. "Let's go inside," he suggests, pulling me toward the jewelry store. A big display of earrings, bracelets and rings sparkles in the window, and normally I'd stop and admire them before moving on.

Now, I'm darn near trembling. "Why are we going in here?" Do I sound nervous? I'm a little nervous.

Forest of Lies

The atmosphere inside the store is quiet, so naturally our appearance results in one of the two employees practically latching onto us. "Hello," she murmurs, warm and inviting. "Please, have a look around. Is there anything you're searching for tonight?"

When she looks at me, all I can do is lift a shoulder while my mouth hangs open. What is this all about? I look to Mitch, confused, since he's the one who dragged me in here in the first place.

"We're only looking around right now," he explains with a charming smile.

I know how it feels to melt in the warmth of his charm, so it's not surprising to find her practically batting her eyes. "By all means, let me know if I can take anything out for you to try on." When Mitch turns his attention to one of the jewelry cases, she winks and gives me a thumbs up. I'm still reeling, unsure of what this all means.

"What are we doing here?" I whisper to Mitch as soon as we're left on our own.

"I don't know." He is being entirely too casual about this as he leads me from one jewelry case to another. "Ah, here we are. There's some pretty nice rings in here."

Rings? A cold sweat chills my skin. It was one thing to talk about marriage on the way down here, but I figured we were discussing it in a strictly hypothetical way. Marriage as a concept, how we both feel about it in general. Suddenly, we're standing in front of a display of sparkling rings and the back of my neck is covered in goosebumps.

"Yes, they're pretty," I offer once I find my voice.

"Any of them you like in particular?"

I can't believe he's asking me this. I told him I wanted to live together first, didn't I? I thought I made that pretty clear. Then again, people live together while they're engaged, too. Is he thinking of turning this trip into a lead-in to his proposal?

And if he were, what would I say? Strange how everything comes together in my head all at once. The charming little store fades into the background. I hardly even feel Mitch's fingers wrapped around mine. Gazing down at the gleaming diamonds, I see the future laid out. I kind of like the way it looks when I imagine Mitch being part of it.

That's why, even though it's still a challenge to catch my breath, I'm able to give thought to his question instead of brushing it off and pleading nerves. "Honestly, I would be too nervous to wear a big ring," I confess while examining a few rings that fit the description. They're pretty – in fact, they're gorgeous, but they're not very practical for somebody who has been known to spend time digging around in dirt and snow for evidence. I would be too afraid of ruining the ring, or of losing it entirely.

"You're not going to get an argument out of me on that," Mitch murmurs close to my ear. When I notice the prices on a few of the very big rings, I understand what he means. I wouldn't want him to put himself in debt over something like this, either. The ring is only a symbol for what really matters, and that's not something we can put a price tag on.

Because I know he won't let me get away with this without choosing something, I point to a square cut solitaire. It's a decent size, not so large that I would feel anxious about maybe catching the stone on something or breaking a prong. I can't believe I'm actually thinking about this. Somebody pinch me.

"That's nice," he agrees, nodding. The gleam from the diamonds reflects in his blue eyes before he looks at me. "That's the kind of style you like?"

"It's much more my speed than one of the bigger rings," I confirm. My heart thuds against my ribs like it's trying to escape my chest, but I do what I can to stay calm. What's he going to do? Is he going to buy it here and now? What would I do if he did?

It feels like an eternity before he chuckles, pulling me close and pressing a kiss against my forehead.

"Okay. I'll keep it in mind." His lips twitch a little when he pulls away. Like he's fighting to hold back a grin and failing horribly.

He's messing around with me. "I cannot believe you," I whisper once he loses the battle and starts laughing. But I'm relieved, really. I want a future with Mitch. I want it more than just about anything. I love knowing he's thinking along these lines. I'm just not sure I'm ready for a ring yet. Soon, but not quite yet.

He's still laughing by the time we reach the sidewalk. "You should've seen the look on your face."

"You know, there are people who would claw your eyes out for playing a trick like that."

"Yes, but you're not one of those women, which is the only reason I would play a little prank like that. I'm pretty sure your soul left your body at one point." Still, his brows draw together like he's concerned. "I didn't take it too far, did I?"

"No, of course you didn't." Still, I shake my head in mock disapproval as we continue through the village, heading for the restaurant. If anything, I love his sense of humor.

Though I can't pretend it's not something of a relief, knowing he'll pick the sort of ring I like when the time comes. When I check in with myself to see how it feels to imagine that day coming, there's nothing but a sense of peace. I can't help but think it would seem completely natural for him to propose and for me to accept. Like that's how it was always meant to be.

29

ALEXIS

It's not until breakfast the morning of our second day in the Vineyard that I know I can't put off the inevitable any longer. Turns out I accidentally packed a great amount of guilt in my bags and I need to fess up.

Mitch must sense my discomfort. After all, he's a pro at reading me. "What's going on? You seem distant this morning." Gazing at me from across the table in the small dining room, he knits his brows together. "What's on your mind?"

I should tell him. I only hope I don't end up ruining any of the happiness we've been marinating in for the past twenty-four hours. I told myself I'd give it a full day before dropping the bomb. At least I'm coming clean instead of sneaking around. Here's hoping he sees it that way.

Setting aside my coffee, I make it a point to look him straight in the eye. "This trip means everything to me. I want you to know that. We needed this, separately and together."

He wipes his mouth with his napkin before sitting back in his chair, hands folded. "Okay. An interesting lead off."

He's not going to make this easy. "But there is a reason I chose the vineyard specifically."

"I had a feeling there was. For an off-the-cuff idea, you seemed pretty sure where you wanted to go."

There's a tinge of disappointment in his voice and right away it sparks bitter shame. "I'm sorry," I whisper. "But this is part of my life, too. Not my work, exactly, but my life. Me, the things that are important to me. And it's important to me that I hunt down any leads regarding Maddie's killer."

His eyes close slowly as he figures out what I've been trying to say. He was there the day I learned Tyler's name. He was at Mom's when I explained things to Captain Felch, trying to get everybody up to speed. "Tyler Mahoney. I should've known. You said he was a lifeguard out here back in the nineties. Once that partial print was identified."

"I'm sorry," I insist when he groans softly. "Please, try to understand. I only want to go to the country club and see if there's any more information I can find about him."

He scrubs his hands over his face, groaning again and leaving me nervous. "I wish you had told me that in the first place." His hands drop into his lap while he releases a heavy sigh. "I wouldn't have minded knowing this was a working trip."

"That's the thing. It's not a work trip. This is our lives I'm talking about now. Yours and mine." My voice is shaking. It's a struggle to keep it low and even for the sake of the inn's owners, who don't need to hear my troubles. "He hasn't left us any notes lately, but that doesn't mean anything. He's still out there, and eventually he's going to get tired of game play. He'll want to up the stakes. I can't sit back and wait for that to happen."

It's torture, sitting here and waiting for him to process this. His disappointment is the hardest thing to bear. My tongue hurts thanks to the way my teeth dig into it, but it's the only way I can keep myself from demanding he tell me what he's thinking. The last thing he needs is me rushing him.

"So what's your plan?" His voice is suspiciously flat now, free of the playful energy I heard before.

"Like I said, I'm hoping maybe somebody at the country club will remember him."

"He worked there almost thirty years ago. I would be surprised if anyone would remember anything."

"You never know. Somebody like that? They give off a vibe. I mean, think about it. A man who ended up preying on adolescents and teenagers? Killing them?" I whisper, looking around to make sure we're not overheard. "He didn't wake up one morning and decide to act like a creep. People tend to remember things like that. The guy who always looked a little longer than he needed to, who was a bit too handsy, you get the idea."

"It's also the off-season," he reminds me. I'm glad he's at least willing to entertain the idea, even if his obvious disapproval stings. "They won't be fully staffed at this time of year."

I hold up a finger. "But the people who are there would be the long-term employees. Not the seasonal hires. I'm banking on that."

He lifts a shoulder, almost dismissive as he picks up his coffee cup. "And as usual, I'm the last one to know."

"Would you have agreed to this trip if I told you straight-out the reason I wanted to come here rather than virtually anyplace else?"

His head bobs once. "Yes. Without a doubt. Because I know how important this is to you. When are you going to stop underestimating me?"

"I guess I didn't want to be accused of being obsessed."

His gaze softens before he lowers it to the table. "If there's anything worth being obsessed about, it's finding your sister's killer. Especially if he happens to be the person stalking us."

"I see your point. And from now on, I promise I'll be more upfront in the first place." He draws his lips into a thin line, fiddling with his fork rather than looking at me. "But Mitch, this is my life. This will never not be important to me, and I am not going to give up until I get my hands on him. I need to know he is put away, once and for all. I am not going to stop until I find him. And I'll do it alone if I have to. It's up to you whether you want to be part of it or not."

"That's quite an ultimatum." I wish I could read what's behind his eyes when they meet mine. He looks troubled, though he sounds less disapproving than he did before.

"It's not an ultimatum. It's a choice, that's all. Do you want to come with me or not? Because I'm going to go, either way."

"Of course, I want to go with you. I sort of have a vested interest in this, remember." I knew he would come around. I only hope he understands why I felt the need to be secretive about this. I didn't want the

Forest of Lies

dark cloud hanging over us all throughout our stay. Now that it's all out in the open, though, I can do my digging, then get back to what the trip was supposed to be about in the first place.

There's not a cloud in the sky when we step outside, and I admire the beautiful morning and the tang of the sea air before following Mitch to the truck. He's still a little quiet, but rather than press him on it I decide to give him his space to think things out. He doesn't need me on his back, demanding he come around and lighten up ... even if that's sort of what I want to beg him to do. Then again, there's really not much about this errand that's fun or exciting, either. It would be unfair for me to force him to pretend he's happy for my sake.

The country club is a ten minute drive from where we're staying, and I'm grateful Mitch seems to have come around a little bit more by the time we turn down a wide, tree-lined boulevard leading up to the clubhouse. It's even more impressive in person than it is in the photos on the club's website, with its towering columns and immaculate landscaping. The exterior's light gray paint looks fresh, and there isn't so much as a smudge on any of the windows that allow for a peek inside the building once we've parked and are on our way inside. There are only a handful of cars in the employee lot off to the side of the building. I can imagine it feels a little desolate around here at this time of year. At least I know the people I talk to won't be too busy to answer a few questions.

Before we go inside, however, I stop and face Mitch. "I want you to know something." He lifts his brows in silent expectation while I fumble around, trying to find the words. "This is the last thing I want to do today. I would much rather focus completely on you. But I need to end this, too. Because if I don't, I'm always going to be looking for him wherever I go. And I don't want to live that way. I don't want to always wonder what he's doing, if he is hunting for his next victim. And if I let him slip through my fingers … "

I don't have a chance to finish before Mitch touches his fingers to my lips and shakes his head. "I get it. You don't have to explain anymore. And when you put it that way, I would feel just as guilty as you would if he hurt or killed somebody else and you weren't able to hunt him down because of me. I don't want to stand in the way. But I would appreciate honesty upfront rather than after the fact. That's all I ask for."

"And I'll give you that from now on," I promise before standing on tiptoe to kiss him. He tastes like coffee and maple syrup. "Now. Do you want to help me catch this guy?"

He lowers his brow while a soft growl rumbles in his chest. "You have no idea how ready I am."

30

ALEXIS

"I feel like I'm too poor to be here." Mitch's tight whisper leaves me chuckling, though I can't pretend I don't relate. I'm almost afraid to breathe the rarefied air in the grand, historic building. On our way to the front desk, we pass a room full of memorabilia. Black and white photos line the walls. I would love to do a little digging in there, though I make it a point to temper my expectations just the same. I'm not going to find my smoking gun here. It would be nice if I did, but I have to be realistic. If I can find a single person who remembers Tyler, that will be a win in my book.

Of course, I would love it to be more than that.

Mitch surprises me by doing the talking when we reach the desk. Right away, I understand his process when he props his elbows on the long counter and offers the middle-aged woman sitting behind it the sort of smile that magically raises the temperature in the room. "Hi. We're in from out of town, doing a little research on a man we believe was once employed here at the club. Do you think you could help us with that?"

She arches an eyebrow, looking him up and down. "It depends. Are you the police?" she asks, but there's no hostility behind the question. Only a touch of suspicion, and I guess I can't blame her for that.

"I am with the FBI," I admit, reaching into my pocket for my badge. I didn't want to flash it around unless forced to do so, and the woman's eyes widen slightly when she sees it. "I'm helping with a series of cases stretching back a few decades. We have reason to believe the man involved was employed here as a lifeguard back in the nineties. It was the fingerprints that were taken for his employment which first put a name to him. Until then, we had no idea who we were dealing with. I was hoping there might be someone working here who was around back then, that they might remember him."

The way she frowns doesn't give me much confidence. "You said it was back in the nineties?" She purses her lips, then blows out a sigh. "There aren't many people here from around that time."

She turns to the laptop on her desk and begins typing while murmuring more to herself than to us.

"Our groundskeeper has been here since the late eighties, if I remember correctly."

Mitch and I exchange a glance while I remind myself not to get my hopes up. A handful of people in matching button-down shirts and dark slacks pass through the lobby, but beyond a few curious looks they continue on. It's so quiet here, I feel like I need to whisper. Almost like a church.

"Here we are." She looks up from the screen. "Ed Fleming has been our groundskeeper since eighty-eight. He's here today. I think he said something about organizing the tool shed."

After finding out where that is, we head back outside. The shed is behind the clubhouse, and the doors are open to reveal a white-haired man who looks to be in his early seventies moving around, whistling softly. His posture is slightly stooped but he moves smoothly, almost gracefully for a man his age.

"Mr. Fleming?" I make sure to sound friendly and casual as we approach. Nothing gets a person to clam up quicker than finding out they're talking to an agent. I introduce myself, and Mitch does the same before I explain what we're looking for. "Do you remember anybody named Tyler Mahoney? I understand it's been a long time, but —"

The old man holds up a gnarled hand before adjusting his thick glasses. "No need. I know exactly who you're talking about. I haven't thought about him in a long time. He's not exactly someone I enjoyed being around."

"Seeing as how you recognize the name right away," Mitch murmurs, "am I wrong to guess he made a strong impression on you?"

The man shakes his head with a humorless chuckle. "No, son, you're about the farthest from wrong you could possibly be. He made a very poor impression on me, but then he did on a lot of people."

I am practically vibrating as I try to absorb this. "What do you remember about him?"

"Oh, you know. There were few concrete reasons for me not to like him. It was more like a feeling, you know. I got a bad feeling." He rubs a hand across the back of his neck while the deep lines in his face deepen further. "He's not the kind of fella you want to leave alone with your sister, if you get what I mean. But he could be charming, that's for sure. Plenty of people around here liked him."

"Not you," I add for him.

"No. Not me. I figured I was overly suspicious since I seem to be the only person who thought there was anything ... off about him."

Forest of Lies

Mitch glances my way before asking, "Did he ever give you any concrete reasons not to trust him?"

I watch his body language closely. It doesn't seem like he's trying to hide anything, and I can't imagine why he would in the first place. At the same time, he seems reluctant to talk. I can't understand why that would be.

"It's been a long time," he says with a sigh after a few silent moments. "But he would sometimes hang around a little too close to the girls when they were laying out with their friends by the pool or on the beach. I'd walk past and see him staring at them. I used to think to myself, I hope nothing happens to any of the kids who are swimming, because they'd be in big trouble with the lifeguard busy ogling some young girls."

None of this exactly surprises me, but it's also not much to go on. "Would you recognize him if you saw him today, do you think? Can you describe what he looked like back then?"

His faded gray eyes light up. "I can do better than that." He moves surprisingly quickly for a man of his age, but then I guess he spends enough time on his feet to keep in shape. I practically have to trot to keep up with him as he leads us back into the clubhouse and straight to the room I noticed earlier. The entire history of the country club is on display here, from a time when ladies wore ankle-length dresses to play tennis through the present time.

"Here he is." Ed comes to a stop at one of the photos hanging on the wall. It's a long, full-color shot featuring a few dozen adolescent kids standing in two rows on the beach, dressed in swimsuits. It reminds me of a school picture, and Ed explains, "This was a swim class from the summer of ninety-three. If I remember correctly, that was Mahoney's first year here."

My interest spikes as I step up closer to the glass so I can study the photo behind it. "That's him?" I whisper, my voice trembling as I stare into the flat eyes of the man who would go on to murder my sister and blow my life apart in another decade's time.

"Sure enough. A bunch of the girls had crushes on him. Some of their mothers did, as well," Ed informs us with no small amount of dry disapproval. "That was before."

"Before?" Mitch asks.

I turn away from the photo to find Ed scowling. "There's a reason he didn't work here too far into his second season. I would've fired him a long time before he ran off if it were up to me."

My skin is tingling. Thoughts race around my brain, questions, theories. I'm getting closer to him. I know

Forest of Lies

I am. "So he ran off? He gave no one any indication of why or where he was going?"

He's staring at the photo, practically burning holes through it. "To tell you the truth, I get the feeling the owners back then were glad to see him go. They didn't want to ask too many questions." Something close to hatred passes over his weathered face. "First, there were a handful of members who decided they didn't want their kids coming around here anymore. A few families left the club altogether. One or two of them were local, too, not the summer people you get every year."

His gaze slides my way, the corners of his mouth tipping downward. "Then there was that one girl who ran off. Just vanished into thin air. Cops tried to say she must've run away with a boyfriend, since she told her best friends there was some older guy she was interested in that summer."

Mitch swallows hard, while I fight to breathe. He was right here. He was hunting here and he had a very full, busy hunting ground.

"This is probably a stupid question," Mitch murmurs, "but were the police ever involved? That you were aware of, I mean?"

The old man scoffs, and I sort of figured he would. This is a familiar story. "Please. Around here, people like to keep things like this quiet. Old families, old money, that's the way of it. The parents swore she would never run away, but the police don't always want to listen. They get an idea in their head and that's it. The club kept all the rumors about Tyler quiet to keep the membership numbers up."

My hands tremble as I reach for my phone, sliding it from my pocket and opening the photo app. I hold the phone close to the picture, centering Tyler's face in the frame. Young, sort of rugged looking — someone who spent time outdoors. He had an almost roguish smile that I could only imagine appeared disarming to countless unwitting people. Like that poor girl who told her friends she was interested in an older man. How many victims did he claim here?

At least now, I have a face to hold in my head when I think of him. When I imagine him looming over my sister, while the last of her life drained away, I can see who she saw.

I can imagine bringing him to an end in one way or another.

31

ALEXIS

"Thank you for doing that with me." On the way back to the inn, I reach out and rub Mitch's shoulder. "I'm sorry we had to take any of our time to do that."

"You don't have to be sorry."

All I can do is raise a skeptical eyebrow, thinking back on his disappointment earlier. I guess he understands the direction my thoughts have taken, because he scowls once we've stopped at a red light.

Turning to me, looking me straight in the eyes, he says, "He's been getting away with it all this time. You and I both know what more than likely happened to that girl Fleming described. And who knows, there could have been other kids he didn't go quite so far with."

"The ones whose families left," I murmur, my heart sinking.

"Exactly. It's time to put a stop to him. All I ask is that you're careful. I mean it," he insists when my knee-jerk response is to placate him. "I want you to be careful. He's like a rabid animal. And he's been at this for a long time. He's not going to like being disturbed."

Now is not the time to remind Mitch I've made this my career, so I keep my thoughts to myself in favor of offering a smile. "I've got this. I'm just glad to know I have you on my side."

"Always." We continue to drive to the inn, where Mitch parks in one of the reserved spaces. On the way inside, I try to change the subject, going over possible dinner choices. It's still too early for lunch, but we both enjoy looking ahead, reviewing the restaurant's menu, getting a feel for the vibe. Exploring, in other words. We are a couple of explorers.

"I mean, seafood seems like the most obvious choice," Mitch points out once we're inside, crossing the cute lobby with its nautical themed decor — lighthouses, anchors, and the like.

"Miss Forrest?" The older man at the desk—one of the inn's owners, if memory serves—waves at us from across the room before we can head upstairs. "I have a message here for you."

Incredible. Moments ago, I was on the verge of imagining a seafood feast for tonight's dinner. Now, a sick feeling washes over me. I can't shake the sense of a pair of headlights bearing down on my frozen form. Mom? Dad? Did something happen to them?

I shake myself out of it quickly and go to the desk, where the man holds out a folded piece of paper. Heavy cardstock by the feel of it.

"He dropped this off for you," the man explains. I notice it's sealed shut with a single piece of clear tape, which I carefully remove before unfolding.

Five words. That's all I see before me, written carefully in block letters.

I'm closer than you think.

"You have to be kidding." Of course, Mitch is behind me, reading over my shoulder. The added pressure of his hands squeezing my shoulders barely registers in my conscious mind, which is now spinning, reeling.

"Who left this?" I whisper, unable to pry my eyes from the print. "Can you describe him?"

"... I don't know," he sputters. "An older man? Maybe in his fifties? He wore a red ball cap and big sunglasses. I didn't get a really good look at his face."

None of this comes as a surprise. What does come as a surprise is his presence here on the island. It has to be Tyler. Who else could it be? He knows exactly where we are, and he waited until we were out to leave his little message.

Where is he now?

Focus. This is not the time to let my thoughts and fears spiral unchecked. My spine stiffens before I lift my chin, forcing myself to think of this as an agent and not as a victim. I hate that word. That is not who I am. "Do you have security cameras around here?" I ask, and now my voice is firm.

"Sure." The poor man is shaking as he gestures toward the camera positioned above his head, pointing at the desk. "Whoever checks in or visits gets picked up on the feed."

"I need to see the footage from when this man came in. Please, it's very important," I insist, reaching for my badge and placing it on the counter to drive the point home. It has its intended effect.

"I'm not normally inclined to do this ..." He waves me behind the counter so I can join him in front of an older model monitor which reveals a live feed of the lobby. The camera picks up Mitch as he stands on the other side of the counter, and the image is clear. I have hope that I'll be able to see something that might help identify Tyler as he looks now.

My hopes don't last long. Once we go back around thirty minutes to his arrival, the best I can see is his plain ball cap and the bulky coat he's wearing. He lifts his head once or twice, but the sunglasses conceal much of his face, and the shadow from the brim of his cap does the rest.

He knew there was a camera. He knew he might be identified. He has thought all of this through down to the last detail.

Hot, frustrated tears threaten to fill my eyes before Mitch jumps into action. "Why don't we head up to the room?" he suggests. Turning his attention to the nearly petrified man behind the desk, he asks, "Would it be possible to get some hot tea?"

"Certainly. I can bring a pot up to the room." If anything, he seems glad to have something to do – and an excuse to leave us on our own, since it seems we're making him uncomfortable. It's not his fault. He didn't sign up for this anymore than we did.

My feet are heavy as I climb the stairs. There are so many questions I want to ask that man, questions I would have asked if my head wasn't spinning.

Tyler is here. He knows where I am. It's not enough to stalk me around Broken Hill. Exactly how long has he been following me, and how far has he tracked me?

"I'm sorry." Misery is starting to replace fear by the time I sink into one of the rocking chairs in front of the fire. I'm strangely sore, and it occurs to me my muscles are clenching thanks to the sudden stress. "I'm so sorry this is happening."

Mitch folds his arms, staring at the flames. "Don't you dare say that," he growls without looking my way. A glance up at him reveals his tight jaw, flared nostrils, his eyes that are now narrowed into slits. "You didn't do any of this. This isn't your fault."

"If it weren't for him knowing I'm onto him …"

"He is responsible for this. Not you." Giving me a sharp look, he mutters, "Understood?"

"Understood." Though it doesn't help. It doesn't help a thing. We are due to stay another two nights, yet now I can't imagine feeling safe here another minute. He's here. Watching. And we don't even even know who to look for, since we haven't gotten a good look at his face.

Or have we?

Mitch watches as I pull up my phone, then pull up the photo from earlier. The one I took at the country club. "What are you doing?" He stands beside me, watching as I upload the photo to an app on my phone.

"I've used this once or twice before," I explain, tapping the screen. "It can help in cases of missing persons. Age progression. What they might look like now."

And this morning, the app will hopefully show me what Tyler Mahoney could look like today. "It's not foolproof, but maybe it will help the clerk identify him. I need to try something. Anything."

"You don't have to explain yourself to me." Mitch runs a hand in circles over my back as we wait for the app to work its magic. In no time at all, the image of a young, smiling Tyler, turns into a slightly fleshier, weathered, older man. There are brackets around the mouth, slight jowls, thinning hair. Granted, the hat would cover that, but I'm hoping something in his face will jog recognition.

There's a soft knock at the door. Mitch crosses the room and opens it to accept the tray of tea. "Can you please take a look at this?" I ask, jumping up from the chair suddenly enough to make the poor owner back up a few steps. "Did the man who left that note look anything like this? I understand a lot of his face was concealed."

He pulls on a pair of glasses, squinting and tipping his head from one side to the other as he studies the image. "The shape of the mouth is familiar," he decides. "And he did have those lines around his mouth. There was a dimple in his chin like there is in this picture."

"Thank you," Mitch murmurs. "You've been a big help."

"I just wish I could do more." The poor guy sounds torn between sympathy and concern. I'm sure that concern is for himself and his business, and I can't blame him. This is a peaceful place, especially at this time of year. Nobody expects to end up embroiled in a situation related to the FBI.

Once Mitch closes the door to leave us on our own again, he pours a cup of tea and drops two lumps of sugar in the cup before directing me back to the rocking chair, then pressing a hand against my shoulder to make me sit down. "You're going to drink this, and you're going to calm down, and then we're going to figure out what to do."

"If he's here on the island, I have to find him." This sweet, strong tea is a welcome pleasure, though I can't really enjoy it. It helps to thaw the ice in my veins, though, and that alone is enough.

"You have to do no such thing. I need to get you out of here," he decides, already on his way across the room to where we left our suitcases in the closet.

It looks like our trip is over. Is there anything Tyler won't destroy?

32

ALEXIS

"We went to a FedEx shipping center on the island, and I sent the note off to the crime lab." Taking a seat on the edge of the bed, I rub the bridge of my nose with my thumb and forefinger. Not that it will do much to ward off the headache that's been brewing ever since I first read that note. "But there's no telling how long it will take for them to find anything, and I'm sure most of the prints on the card belong to the man behind the front desk, anyway."

Captain Felch groans. "It sounds like you need to cut your trip short. I'm really very sorry it turned out this way."

My teeth grind at the thought. "I don't think we should cut the trip short."

Forest of Lies

It's the funniest thing. Captain Felch is hours away from where Mitch currently packs his things, yet they manage to speak in unison. "What?" they both snap.

"I'm not leaving," I insist. "Captain, I'm putting you on speaker." Because really, I don't feel like arguing with both of them separately. It will probably be easier to handle them at the same time.

"Can you please talk some sense into her?" Mitch asks him while folding a sweater that was folded in the first place. He's nervous, and I understand why, but that doesn't change my mind.

"Alexis, it is not a good idea for you to stay on the island," the captain tells me in a grave voice. "I'm not trying to ruin your trip or rain on your parade or however you'd like to describe it. This is important."

"You don't need to tell me how important it is. Trust me, I understand." It's only that we have differing opinions on where the importance lies. He believes it's important for me to get out of here to save my hide. I think it's more important to catch Tyler here and now if possible.

Mitch tosses the sweater into the suitcase a little harder than necessary. "Then why are you being so stubborn? If you understand how important it is to get out of here and keep yourself safe?"

"What am I supposed to do? Let him dictate my entire life? We're supposed to be here together, having a little vacation. I'm supposed to call that off because of him? He wins. Don't you get that?"

"He also wins if he lures you into the open, unable to defend yourself." I can practically see the captain's concerned expression. I've certainly seen it enough times, paired with the strain I now hear in his voice.

"And I suppose none of my training comes into account at a time like this?" I ask, looking at Mitch.

"Alexis." He sits next to me, covering one of my hands with his. Normally, his touch quiets down some of the noise in my head, but this isn't one of those times. The dull roar doesn't lessen one bit. "This has nothing to do with confidence in your training or your abilities. This has to do with that psycho following us more than four hours from home and leaving that message when he knew we weren't here. He's watching us right now. Do you honestly think we could enjoy the rest of our time here, looking over our shoulders? And don't tell me you wouldn't be on the lookout, either. I know I certainly will."

He's not wrong. As it is, every sound I hear from downstairs makes my heart seize. Every creaking floorboard becomes Tyler's approaching footsteps. There's no way I would get a wink of sleep tonight, that much is for sure.

Though now that I know the lengths he's willing to go to, how am I supposed to get a wink of sleep at home? There's never any knowing when he's chosen to watch. To stalk.

"You do not need to be there," Captain Felch insists. "They're going to find prints on that note to match Tyler's, and then — "

"And then what?" I demand. "I already know it was him. Who else would it have been? That won't get me any closer to him."

"Waiting around with a target on your back isn't going to do you any favors, either." He sounds rather sharp, exasperated. I'm sure some of that has to do with worrying over Pete, who is still missing. I'm almost sorry to bother him with my concerns, but then he's the one who called to check in and make sure I was actually enjoying myself down here. Boy, didn't he get a surprise.

"I get it," I groan, sighing heavily. They have me between a rock and a hard place. "It's just that ... how does it look? He's going to watch us load our things into the truck and head home. What message does that send? He's winning. He is calling the shots and I hate the idea of giving in."

"I know." Mitch's fingers tighten around my hand before he leans in, touching his forehead to my temple. "I don't want to go, either. I don't want this monster thinking he has an ounce of power over us. But I am not going to sit around here waiting for his next move, either. And I am not letting you put yourself in danger. You are too important."

My teeth dig into my tongue, since nobody needs to hear what is dangerously close to tumbling out of my mouth. I hate this. I hate that man, I hate what he's done, I hate the fact that this is a game for him. That he's deriving enjoyment from this. I hate more than anything knowing how he'll laugh to himself over it. Feeling like he is calling the shots, pulling the strings, making us dance to his tune.

"You're going to find him." Captain Felch is grim with determination. "He's taking risks. Chasing the thrill. And I'm sure you know that when a person like him loses sight of their safety because they're busy seeing how much they can get away with, that's when they start making mistakes."

I know he's right. All of my training tells me so.

What he doesn't understand and never could is how all of that training flies out the window when a situation like this gets personal.

Then again, maybe he does get it. Now that his nephew is missing, he must understand on a deeper level the anxiety, the panic, the sense of helplessness. It's one thing to witness a situation from a law enforcement perspective, but another when it's personal.

I'm tilting at windmills here. None of my arguing is going to make much of a difference when nobody is listening to me. Besides, Captain Felch is right. Tyler's becoming brazen. He's so bent on announcing himself, making sure we know he's in control. He's bound to take things too far. When he does, I have to be ready for him.

"Okay." That single word is heavy. It's not easy to say. "Let's pack up and get moving, I guess."

While I pack against my will, I envision Tyler's face. Eventually, I'm going to have to turn the tables. To become the watcher instead of the one who's being watched. I need to take control of the situation.

Or else my life will never be mine.

33

ALEXIS

"You're sure this is okay? I don't want to make things any worse for your sister."

Captain Felch runs a hand through his hair before gazing out through the driver's side window of the patrol car. I would swear there's more gray in it than there was last week at this time. Looking toward his sister's humble home, he sighs. "It isn't as if any of this has been easy. If you can find something none of the officers around here could find, it could mean the break we've been looking for. That's what matters more than anything."

"And it's all right that I'm here while Becky is at work?" Frankly, I can't imagine how she manages to focus at a time like this, but then I doubt the electric company would be very sympathetic if she didn't have money to pay her bill. There's a fine line a person has to walk at a time like this. The world doesn't stop turning even in the face of extreme personal tragedy.

"If anything, I think she would rather you look through Pete's room while she's not here," he confesses. "It's not easy for her to witness that sort of thing. It's still his room. His things. He wouldn't like anyone going through them." His voice catches before he stares straight through the windshield, taking a deep breath before adding, "Let's hope you find something."

Strange, but I'm behaving like Becky now as I pull on a pair of latex gloves while walking the short pathway up to the tiny house. By the time we reached Broken Hill yesterday, I was determined not only to put more energy into locating Tyler, but to help with Pete's case. I need to feel like I can accomplish something, like I'm not always chasing my tail with nothing to show for it. I have no doubt the officers working under the captain know what they're doing, but I have a certain skill set they don't possess.

It was Mitch who left me thinking about doing this. "You never know. There might be something hidden in his room, like there was in Camille's." He was referring to Camille Martin, the girl whose kidnapping brought me back to my hometown. A good kid, much like Pete, but even the most trustworthy kid can have secrets. In Camille's case, that involved an illicit relationship with one of her teachers. While that relationship had nothing to do with her kidnapping, it helped remove a predator from the school. I'm hoping to find a secret or two in Pete's room, something to point us in the right direction.

There is something distinctly sad and haunted about the home I step into alone, and for a second, I wrestle with the sense of being an invader. An interloper destroying the peace. Only when I remind myself the peace was disturbed last week by some unnamed, unknown person am I able to move deeper into the house.

It's obvious Becky hasn't placed much of a priority on housekeeping, not that I blame her. Who could be bothered to worry about the dishes in the sink when their son is missing? I hesitate on my way past the kitchen, wanting to help clean up if only to make Becky's life a little easier, but that's not my place. It's not what I'm here for, either. I press on and soon reach a cheap wooden door. First room on the right, according to the captain. Easing it open, I'm treated to the sight of a surprisingly neat and tidy little room. Not at all what I would have expected from a fourteen-year-old boy, but then Pete is the exception to the rule in many ways.

Forest of Lies

Has he been hiding something? Pushing aside everything I've learned so far, I assess the room through the eyes of a professional. Immediately, I'm drawn to the dozens upon dozens of books crammed into a set of bookshelves that over time have started to sag under the weight. A smile tugs at my mouth as I examine the titles. I recognize a few of them as having come from Mitch's store thanks to a sticker in the top right corner of the cover. He did say a while back that he wanted to start stocking more fantasy titles, and it appears Pete took advantage of that.

I need to focus up. Instead of admiring the titles, I begin removing the books – carefully, keeping them in order row by row. Some people take their bookshelves very seriously, and what might look like random chaos to the casual observer could be a carefully devised system. I fan the pages of each book, hoping for … what? Something hidden. Like the drawing Benji found, only something that could give me insight into Pete's thoughts, into something he might have hidden.

One by one, I clear then refill the shelves. By the time I've reached the bottom shelf, I sit cross legged on the floor, feeling doubtful and even a little guilty for not having found something useful.

That is, until I find the notebook. I wouldn't have noticed it otherwise if I had only casually examined the shelves. He hid it between the front cover and dust jacket of a large, thick hardback. With the books lined up neatly, it was easy to miss.

I lay the book on the floor in front of me. One of those old marble copybooks, but much thinner than the ones I'm used to seeing. A lot of the pages have been ripped out, leaving maybe half of the book behind. It looks like Pete might have torn out old schoolwork – some of the jagged bits of paper still contain pieces of dates stretching back to last year.

On the first empty page, Pete began his journal. The opening entry dates back six months.

Dad moved out for good today. Now it's real. Before, he was just staying with Brittany or at a hotel, but now they're really finished. The house feels emptier, and it makes me sad, but I'm also kind of relieved. If he's not here, they're not screaming at each other. But Mom still cries. It is the worst feeling in the world, hearing her crying when there's nothing I can do.

Poor kid. I can relate, heaven knows. He took his parents' separation to heart, the way any intelligent, sensitive kid his age would.

A few days later, there was another entry.

Mom says I have to get used to spending some nights with dad and Brittany, since that's what the judge will decide I have to do anyway. Dad keeps telling me he wants us to still be close, and I kind of want to tell him we haven't been close in a long time, but we'd only end up fighting more. He would probably blame it on Mom, too.

As days passed, the entries became more sporadic. Sometimes a week would pass, sometimes there would be two entries in a single day.

I can't wait to go back home. I get so tired of pretending.

She told dad I have to start sleeping in the living room from now on since my room will be the nursery for the baby.

She keeps talking about Dad starting fresh. One time, she was looking right at me when she said it. I knew what she meant. She doesn't want me here.

She hates me. I don't know what to do.

"Oh, no," I whisper. There's a sick feeling in my stomach and a cold, sticky sweat coats the back of my neck. That entry was dated two weeks back and is the second to last in the journal. The final entry isn't really an entry at all, but rather a series of seemingly random characters written on two rows of the lined paper. I stare at it, wondering what they could mean, before realizing I could be looking at a username and password.

But for what? Was this a means of reminding himself ... or leaving clues for whoever found the journal? It's not very helpful without a clue as to which site he was using.

A stroke of insight leaves me reaching for my phone, pulling off one of my gloves to google the username, **L3g0l@s**. Legolas is a character from *Lord of the Rings*. I've never read the books or watched the movies, but I recognize the name from various memes.

Right away, an account pops up as the first search result. YouTube. He created a YouTube account under that username. Pete's face fills the thumbnail image, almost eerie thanks to the glow from his laptop screen. I tap the link and open the app to play the video. It's the only one he ever uploaded, dated two days before his disappearance. My heart is in my throat and I'm holding my breath by the time playback begins.

"I've got to tell somebody." His voice is a whisper, like he's trying to keep a secret. I recognize the background—he was in his own room, and considering how dark it was, Becky was more than likely at work at the time. Yet still he whispered. He was ashamed of something.

"I don't know if anybody will ever see this, and I guess it's better if you don't, but there's nobody I can talk to about it. My dad's fiancee is crazy, and she hates me, and I'm scared if I say anything she'll do something to hurt my mom."

He sat here, in this room, making this confession. Alone, in the dark, reaching out to no one. He's trembling, and his voice breaks before he raises his left arm and pulls back the short sleeve of his t-shirt.

"She did this." I bring the phone close to my face to study the pair of small, round wounds on the underside of his arm. "I woke up on Saturday night when I was visiting. Dad was still working at the bar. Brittany had a cigarette and she held my arm down and told me it was my fault she got in a fight with Dad over the bedrooms, because he doesn't think I should have to sleep on the couch. She told me if I fought back, she would say I tried to hurt her and the baby. And then … she burned me." He releases a whimper, so broken and painful it brings tears to my eyes. "She said it's my fault, that they're happy when I'm not here, but I always get in the way. And she's not gonna let me break them up."

He then stands and turns to the side before lifting his shirt to his ribs. I wince at the sight of a bruise there, a few days old by the looks of it. "And then she kicked me, and she told me if I ever tell anyone, she'll say it was Mom who did it to me. And nobody's gonna believe me because I just want my parents to get back together, so I'm making things up. Only I'm not. it's really happening, and I don't know what to do, and I'm scared if she has a baby, she'll do it to them, too. She's crazy. But if I tell anybody, I'll get Mom in trouble. I don't know what to do."

He sits back down and runs a hand through his hair, though it only flops back onto his forehead. "Anyway, I can't keep it all in. Maybe I'll make another video."

He didn't. He never got the chance.

The only sound is that of my own breathing as I absorb and process this. Brittany's image flashes in my mind's eye. Rubbing her belly, comforting her grieving fiance. She struck me as a little self-absorbed, but I brushed it off as concern for the baby at a stressful time.

Now, armed with this notebook and with Pete's video, I see everything in a different light.

Captain Felch is waiting for me by the car when I emerge from the house. When his face falls, I know mine must reveal my concern—and horror. "You found something." It's not a question.

"I found something," I tell him, and not without regret. "We need to look at Brittany. Immediately."

34

ALEXIS

"You can't be anywhere near this." It's strange, talking to the captain this way, no matter how it needs to be done. He's anxious, pacing his office, grinding his teeth loud enough that I can hear them when he passes close to me. "We can't afford to make any mistakes. You can watch the feed, but you know that's it."

"I realize that." He's a little sharp, but all things considered, I let it go.

"I know what I'm doing," I remind him, though even as I say it, I'm fighting the surge of emotion that fills me whenever I remember the way Pete sounded in that video. I've watched it countless times now, and between that and ceaselessly poring over the journal entries, there is nothing even remotely resembling neutrality anymore.

Still, that is not something I can reveal during the interview. I've painstakingly prepared my questions, leaving nothing to chance. There is no room for emotion here. Pete needs me to play the game for as long as it takes.

A brief rap on the door precedes, the appearance of one of the deputies assigned with bringing Brittany and Andrew in for questioning. "They're in room two," he announces. I thank him while the captain pulls up the feed from that room on the monitor beside his desk.

What a surprise. She's stroking her belly, singing softly between sips from a water bottle. The captain grunts and mutters a few choice words under his breath before turning away. "I can't look at her."

"You don't have to. You don't even have to listen," I remind him gently, quietly. It would probably be better if he didn't, though I can understand his determination. I would feel the same way in his shoes.

I can't stay in here with him forever, and besides, this is something I've looked forward to ever since leaving the house with Pete's journal. Anticipation quickens my pulse as I approach the small room and knock softly on the door before entering. I have to look friendly, polite.

"Thank you both for coming in," I offer before closing the door behind me. Andrew McClintock paces in tight circles in the far corner of the room, his arms folded, his face drawn and gray. I wonder if he's slept more than an hour at a time in the past week. At least three days worth of stubble cover his cheeks and jaw, but it does little too conceal how sunken his face has become. The amount of silver in his beard ages him dramatically, and I remember Becky mentioning he dyes his hair.

"Tell me you found something," he pleads in a voice choked with desperation. "Anything. I can't take this."

My heart goes out to him, something I don't have to conceal. "Mr. McClintock, believe me when I say we're doing everything we can. And it does seem as though we've uncovered some new information, hence the reason for bringing you in."

"Oh, finally. Somebody's doing their job." Brittany clicks her tongue in disapproval. "I mean, Broken Hill is not a very big place. How long could it take to find a missing kid?"

"I understand your frustration." Taking a seat across from her, I offer the closest thing to a smile I can manage. "Hopefully, we can come closer to understanding what Pete was going through around the time of his disappearance."

"Going through?" Andrew drops his arms to his sides. "What was he going through? Are you telling me Becky–"

His mouth snaps shut when I shake my head firmly, then turn to his fiancée. "Brittany, tell me more about your relationship with Pete."

She lifts a shoulder. "I've already told you everything. He's a good kid. He never gave anybody any trouble."

"You're sure about that? He never gave anyone any trouble? Including you?"

"What are you trying to say?" Andrew drops into the chair beside hers and takes her hand in his. "This is pathetic. You can't go around accusing innocent people all because you can't find the real threat."

Rather than address him, I keep my attention focused on Brittany. "Is it true you argued over whether Pete's bedroom at your home should be converted to a nursery? Is it true he no longer had a bedroom in your home?"

The look they exchange speaks volumes. Surprise on his side, and maybe something close to fear on hers. "How did you know about that?" Andrew asks. I notice he doesn't sound as defiant now.

"Is it true you blamed Pete for that argument?" I continue, studying Brittany's reaction. The way she shifts her weight, the flaring of her nostrils, her short, quick breaths.

"I don't know where you're getting any of this," she blurts out. "No, that's not true. I mean, yeah, we talked about the sleeping arrangements ..." She looks to Andrew for help, lifting her brows, silently prodding him. Either he can't chime in or he doesn't want to. All he does is sit, staring at her the way I do.

"Is it true, Brittany, that you threatened Pete with accusing his mother of abusing him if he ever went public with accusations of abuse from you?"

"This is ridiculous!" Andrew shouts, pounding his fist on the table. "I don't know what you're talking about!"

Right on cue, Brittany's eyes well up with tears. "This is insane! He's right, you're just throwing accusations around now because you don't have any evidence and you can't do your job. How is that my fault? Why should I be punished for that?"

"I want you to think long and hard about this." As I speak, I open the folder I brought with me and withdraw the photocopied pages from Pete's journal. "And remember, I would not pull these accusations out of thin air. I have a source. If there weren't some evidence, how would I have known about your fight over the bedroom situation?"

Andrew's mouth falls open – then snaps shut. He must see the truth in what I said.

"He probably told Becky about it." She withdraws her hand from Andrew's and wraps her arms over her belly like she's protecting herself. "That's all it is. He probably went and complained to her."

Andrew turns his head slowly until he's looking her in the eye. "How would he know about it unless you told him? We fought about that before he got to the house. I didn't want him to hear any of it." She can't come up with an answer for that, her cheeks flushing before she averts her gaze.

"This might be of some interest to you both." I fan out the pages containing Pete's entries, but keep the screenshots to myself for now. I would rather not show them to Andrew unless necessary. No need to rub salt in the wound. I'm hoping Brittany doesn't force my hand. "Pete's journal goes back months, and he details the way your relationship went south."

"I knew it! I knew he would do something like this." Tears now stream freely down her cheeks as she sputters her way through playing the victim. "He always hated me. He always blamed me for what happened. I was a wicked stepmother, something like that. He told me he would find a way to split us up! He did!" she insists when Andrew looks up from his son's writing.

Forest of Lies

"Pete wouldn't do that," he chokes out. "That's not him. He only ever wanted to make things better for everybody."

"See? There you go again! Always believing him! What about me?" She's shaking now, sobbing openly, though neither of us has made a move to comfort her.

"Brittany," I murmur, "I wouldn't have brought you in here and made accusations like this if I didn't have proof."

"Proof? What, a bunch of fantasies made up by some kid?" She shoves the papers away from her, barking out another sob. "Please. He would've said anything to split us up and get his parents back together!"

"Why are you talking about him in past tense?" I ask.

Her eyes bulge. "I'm not! I mean, I did, but I'm talking about the past. It only makes sense, right? Don't do that!" She sobs again. "Don't put words in my mouth!"

"Like I said." My fingers tap the screenshots, turned face down for the sake of discretion. "There's more than those pages. Pete created a video describing an encounter the two of you shared. I'm imagining it took place the same day as the argument you had over the sleeping arrangements. Where were you that night, Mr. McClintock?"

He clasps his hands on top of his head, blinking rapidly. The poor man. This is rocking his world. "I guess that would've been a Saturday, right? So I was at the bar. I always stay till closing on Saturday nights, so I don't get home until three or maybe four in the morning."

Meanwhile, I watch Brittany. I watch her slouch in her chair, I watch her shoulders lift until they almost cover her ears. "I know what you did to him that night," I whisper. "He shows it in the video."

"What did you do?" Andrew grips the table, leaning closer to Brittany. "What did you do to my son?"

"Maybe you should leave the room." I look up at the camera, knowing the captain is watching along with at least one or two officers. We might need help in here before much longer.

Brittany reaches for him, but isn't quick enough to touch him before he pulls back. "I didn't do anything! Baby, please! You know me. And you know they're desperate to pin this on somebody, That's all this is, dirty cops. They don't care about the truth. They just want to wrap up their case."

"Are you a smoker, Brittany?"

Her head whips around at my question. "Not since I got pregnant," she snaps. "What, are you going to arrest me for it?"

Without saying a word, I flip over the first screenshot featuring Pete's burns. "He claimed they were from a cigarette," I explain. "Mr. McClintock, I am sorry to make you look at this."

He leans forward like someone punched him in the stomach, almost doubled over. "Oh. Oh, no. What did you do?" he asks Brittany again. "What did you do to my kid?"

"Brittany, that's not the only injury he shows in the video." By now she has covered her face with her hands, rocking back and forth while her sobs fill the room. This is only going to get uglier. "I'm sure whatever happened, it was unintentional."

I have to swallow back the bile that rushes into my throat as I fight to maintain a soothing tone. "I'm sure you didn't mean it, and that it's eating you alive now. The stress can't be good for you or the baby. But there's no undoing this, either. The only way forward is to tell the truth. This could go much easier for you if you do."

Her head swings wildly from side to side. "I didn't … I didn't!"

"But you did hurt him," I remind her, prompting a fresh round of deafening sobs. "Maybe it went too far. It wouldn't be the first time a tragic accident occurred."

"Please …" she weakly pleads from behind her hands. "Stop. I can't take it."

"Let's end all of it," I suggest over her protests. "It will go easier for you if you tell us what we need to know. The court takes that into account."

Meanwhile, all Andrew can do is sit silently and watch this unfold. I can't imagine what he must be going through as Brittany slowly lowers her hands. "I could cut a deal?" she asks in a small, almost childlike voice.

"What did you do?" He stands, holding onto the table like it's the only thing keeping him upright. "Answer me. What did you do? What did you do to my son?"

"I need help in here!" I bark, wedging myself between him and the table where Brittany now cowers in fear.

"What did you do? Where is my son?" he shouts as the door opens and a pair of officers rush in to take hold of him. "My Pete! Where is he? What did you do?"

35

ALEXIS

It isn't more than a half hour before I take a seat again, this time in the presence of Brittany's lawyer. Leonard Schaeffer is vaguely familiar to me, having worked in Broken Hill for as long as I can remember. He didn't defend Russell Duffy, but if memory serves, the lawyer who represented him worked for the same firm at the time. Unlike his former colleague, it doesn't seem that Leonard was thrown onto this case against his will. Brittany called him after asking for her lawyer's presence, thus effectively ending the questioning until he arrived.

The woman sitting across from me is a far cry from the sobbing wreck she was not so long ago. There's an almost cold attachment now — she sits with her hands folded, upright, like a kid in school prepared to deliver a report.

Leonard clears his throat, eyeing the recorder on the table before glancing toward the camera in the corner. "Let's get this over with, Agent Forrest," he murmurs. "I would like to state here and now that my client offers this information in exchange for a plea deal. If my client describes the events which took place and leads you to the remains of the victim, she does so to lessen her sentence in hopes of raising her baby outside of prison."

Yes, she's everyone's vote for Mother of the Year. "That's been understood, and the district attorney is aware of your conditions. They are currently on the premises, observing this confession. Now, Brittany," I continue, turning toward her, "all of this is contingent upon your honesty. We'll need you to take us to Pete's body for the agreement to go into effect. Is that clear?"

Her head bobs before she clears her throat. "I just want to get it over with."

That makes two of us. "Please, then. Tell me what happened the night of Pete's disappearance."

She tucks her hair behind her ears, her hands trembling before she blows out a long breath. It seems to bolster her a little. "He wasn't supposed to be there that night. Andrew was working late, closing up. I told Pete that when he showed up at the house, and he said he was home alone and a little freaked out. Like he wanted to spend the night at our house."

Why would he have wanted to do that when he knew Brittany hated him? Was he that freaked out, being alone in the house at night?

"What did you say?" I prompt.

"I told him his dad wouldn't be home for hours and I didn't feel like giving him the couch, because I was still up watching TV. I told him he had to go home. It wasn't even that far. He gave me a hard time about it, then said he would walk down to the bar. He wanted to see his father. I started getting suspicious."

"About what?"

"It was pretty obvious. He wanted to tell Andrew on me. He wanted to ruin everything. He wasn't a good liar. So I told him I would walk with him – he didn't like that idea, which was when I knew for sure what he planned on doing. So I said I would walk him partway, through the woods since it's pretty dangerous out there at night. I guess he must have believed me, since he didn't argue."

Her voice goes quiet and small. "We reached the woods, and I had to say something. I told him I knew what he was trying to do. He denied it, of course, and I told him I didn't believe him. We started arguing. I was so mad. So frustrated with him. He was always in the way. This was supposed to be my time. The baby, the engagement, everything was going right. He accused me of breaking up his parents' marriage, all the kind of things you would expect a kid to say. And I ... snapped. I just snapped. And I pushed him."

She stares down at her hands, twisting in her lap. "He fell. He hit his head. I knew as soon as I heard it."

"Knew what? Heard what?"

"I heard his head hit a rock or something. You don't forget a sound like that. The way it cracked."

I force myself to control my reaction, but it's not easy. "And then what?"

"What do you think? I panicked. Here I am, pregnant, in the freezing cold and dark. I was freaking out. I didn't know what to do at first. But I had to think about my baby. I had to do what was best for them."

"Meaning what?"

"I covered him up. I did what I could with branches and rocks. It took a long time. And when I was finished, I found this book laying on the ground – I tripped on it, he must have dropped it when he fell. I think it was in his coat pocket, maybe. We weren't far from the river, and I knew he liked to go down there sometimes, so I hid it under some rocks instead of taking it home. I figured somebody could find it there and link it to him. I was only doing what I thought I needed to do for the baby. That's all. I was trying to be a good mother to my child."

By killing another child and covering up the crime. The worst part is, I know she believes what she's saying. I hear it in her voice, I see it in the way her eyes shine. She honestly thinks she did what she had to do.

"Are you saying you buried him close to the place where you hid the book?" I ask.

"It wasn't that close – he took me there once, back when Andrew and I first got together. I was trying to be his friend. He said he used to go there sometimes and read by himself, so I figured it made sense."

"But can you remember where you hid the body?"

She nods slowly. "Sure. I remember where it was. I'll take you there, so long as it means I don't have to go to prison."

I exchange a look with Leonard, who clears his throat. "We're looking for a reduced sentence," he reminds her. "You won't avoid all prison time, but you will get off quite easily, I can assure you of that. A young, pregnant woman, full of hormones …" He lifts an eyebrow in my direction, and I have to swallow my outrage before nodding.

It burns me inside, taking this deal, but without it there would never be closure for Andrew or Becky. Pete is gone now. There's nothing we can do to help him beyond bringing him home. And short of sending the entirety of the Broken Hill Police Department hiking through the woods to find the body, this is the only way of finding him quickly and putting all of it to an end.

Standing, I murmur, "We've confirmed with the family that they are willing to accept this deal, and they're waiting along with a handful of deputies to visit the site."

For the first time since Leonard's arrival, Brittany's face reflects true fear. "Andrew's going to be there? I don't want him there," she whimpers.

"He wants to be there, and it's his right as the father." That's as much as I can manage to choke out before turning away. Leonard whispers a few things to her as we gather our things and prepare to head out to the scene of Pete's resting place.

It's rare for me to dislike my work, but at times like this, it's difficult to find any satisfaction in the truth when the truth is so sad. Captain Felch stands with Becky near his office, and the short nod I give him answers the questions he doesn't dare voice. He takes a slow, deep breath before nodding.

Soon we head out as a group with Brittany carefully guarded by a handful of officers in case either Becky or Andrew lose their grip on themselves.

If I were in their shoes, I doubt I would be able to hold it together.

36

ALEXIS

It's a familiar scene. Yellow caution marks the borders of where a mound of branches and rocks and leaves supposedly mark Pete's makeshift grave. The forensics team is here, along with the deputies and officers who came over from the station. The mood is grim, the task thankless. I stand between the scene and the family, though I hear them behind me. Captain Felch stands beside one of the patrol cars with Becky and Andrew. It seems like this experience has dissolved the tension among them, if only for now. Tragedy has a way of doing that.

Brittany is handcuffed, weeping quietly with only her lawyer to comfort her as the team begins removing one layer of debris after another. We were so close, Benji and me – I can see from where I'm standing the place where he found Pete's book. If anything, I am deeply relieved a book was all he found that day. What if he had accidentally discovered the body? I can't bear the thought. The poor kid will have enough to process now that this is over. Now that we know for sure.

Only a handful of minutes pass before I see it. A sneaker. An ankle. Filthy, soaked thanks to the snow that has fallen and melted, but very visible.

One of the men turns, meets my gaze, and nods.

A sharp cry slices through the air. A howl. "No! Oh, no! Pete!"

Turning, I find Becky slumping in Captain Felch's arms, her shrieks loud enough to make the birds take wing all around us. Andrew kneels beside her, weeping, while she continues her heartbroken wails. "Pete… Pete…" she moans. Andrew takes hold of her while Captain Felch rests a hand on her head, his face a stony mask as he stares at the scene of his nephew's grave.

"Not to make it about me, but I've never felt so useless in all my life." I draw in, then release a deep breath that doesn't do much to soothe my aching heart. "It reminded me so much of Mom, hearing Becky's reaction. It took me right back to the past."

"I'm so sorry. That must've been difficult." Mitch rubs my shoulder, sitting beside me at one of the tables in his café. There aren't any customers on this side of the space this late in the day — most people try to avoid caffeine in the early evening, or at least that's always been my experience. Unless I'm working a case, of course, at which point all bets are off.

"At least the family has closure. I remember hearing somebody say that when Maddie was found. I didn't understand that at the time, but I get it now. There's nothing worse than not knowing."

"I feel bad for the father." When I arch an eyebrow, he shrugs. "I mean, it was bad enough he broke up his marriage over that woman. To find out she murdered his son?"

I see his point. "If not murdered, definitely killed. It's a gray area. The way she makes it sound, it was a tragic accident."

"Which she then covered up."

"Self-preservation – and of course, she would do anything to protect her baby." Though really, I have my doubts. It's easy for a person to come up with an excuse like that after the fact what she described to me sounds more like panicked self-preservation than anything else, with or without the pregnancy hormones her lawyer mentioned.

Forest of Lies

"Mitch? Sorry, this lady has a question." One of Mitch's employees waves our way from behind the register.

"Be right with you." Mitch stands, and it's like he flips a switch somehow. Now he's the charming, affable business owner, when only a moment ago he was the sweet, concerned boyfriend. He has a talent for compartmentalizing that I find enviable. I only thought I was good at it before reacquainting myself with him. The man is a master.

It's a habit, checking my phone when I have a quiet moment to myself. There wasn't much time to go through my inbox while Brittany was being processed and arrangements were made to transport Pete's body to the medical examiner's office for an autopsy. The forensic team's initial analysis confirms Brittany's story. The back of his head was badly injured, and any other damage on the body was most likely done by wildlife small and agile enough to reach the body despite Brittany's attempts at hiding it.

At first, I almost overlook the email from the Boston field office. My former home base.

My body tingles as my finger hovers over the message before opening it. What if I'm reassigned somewhere far away? Just when things seem to be getting better all the time with Mitch. Could I leave the people I love behind with Tyler Mahoney still running around, casting a shadow over all of us? It's almost better not knowing for sure, but there's no running from reality. No matter what the email holds, I have to accept it and find a way to make things work.

Still, I can't breathe as I tap the message, chewing my lip, my insides churning. I am so worried, it takes two or three scans of the text to understand the message.

With this in mind, it's been decided that you will remain in the area to further investigate the presumed serial killer whose cabin you first discovered. I ask that you keep in close touch with my office and that you alert me to any needs which might arise.

"What is it?" I didn't realize Mitch came back until he's practically on top of me, and the concern in his voice tells me I must look like I've seen a ghost.

I can only blurt out a disbelieving laugh. "My transfer came through."

"And?" He drops to one knee beside me, his voice grave with concern. "I can't tell if this is a good or bad thing."

"Good. Very good. I'm staying here. They want me to keep investigating Tyler."

Yet he does not share my joy. At first, his eyes light up and he begins to smile – before familiar lines crease his brow. "So you're telling me things are going to get even more dangerous now you're officially investigating him?"

"This is a good thing," I remind him, taking his face in my hands and staring deep into his beautiful blue eyes. Eyes that are full of hope and concern and equal measure. "It's a very good thing. I get to stay here. With you. Don't tell me you're upset about that," I add, teasing him a little in hopes of dragging a smile from him.

And I succeeded. "It is a good thing," he agrees with a relieved sigh. "I'm not ready to let you go."

"What do you say we go out and get some dinner? My treat." For the first time all day, I feel like things are going to turn out all right. No long-distance relationship, no driving between Broken Hill and wherever the Bureau decides to transfer me. I'm going to stay here for as long as it takes.

"What about that Thai place we passed on the way back into town? Remember, it's maybe fifteen minutes away?" I'm glad to see Mitch feeling a little more positive by the time we are walking to his truck, and I would agree to just about anything to keep him that way. It's a good thing I happen to like Thai food.

"That sounds good. And then … Oh, jeez, I'm going to have to do the inevitable."

He gives me a quizzical sort of look as he opens my door for me. "What's the inevitable? What am I missing?"

"Well, I'm going to have to apologize to my parents and hope they're willing to forgive me for my little childish outburst." I'm still ashamed of how I behaved that morning, and the fact that neither of them has exactly gone out of their way to reach out tell me they might still be a little miffed. Since then, the fire marshall confirmed the fire was the result of arson. I know that was never Tyler's expertise, but there's no way of knowing he hasn't decided to branch out.

I refuse to believe it's a matter of coincidence that somebody burned Dad's trailer to the ground the same day I received a note threatening Mom's life. No way.

"They'll forgive you," Mitch predicts with an easy grin. I wish I shared his confidence.

He must see the worry on my face when he joins me in the truck, because he gets serious. "Hey. You didn't do anything unforgivable. Families fight. That doesn't mean there's no forgiveness. If anything, I would think all three of you would make it a point to stick together after everything you've gone through."

Of course, he's right. "Oh, imagine if they're too busy … together … to think about me. You know what I mean." The thought makes me gag. It doesn't matter that I'm thirty years old. Nobody wants to think about their parents going through a honeymoon phase.

His laughter is gentle. "Maybe we should call first before stopping by? Just in case? We wouldn't want to interrupt anything."

"I'm going to throw up," I warn, which only makes him laugh harder.

"What a shame it's a little too late for them to give you another sibling."

"Forget getting sick. I'm going to jump out of the truck."

"Okay, all right, sorry." He doesn't look or sound sorry, but then I wouldn't expect him to. I can even laugh a little.

"Really, I'm glad for them. It's just a strange thought, staying in the house with both of them again. I haven't done that in so long. The next thing I know, they'll be demanding I'm home by curfew."

This time, he doesn't laugh. A glance his way reveals a serious, thoughtful expression as he drives us down Main Street. "Okay, what gives?" I finally have to prompt after two blocks of silence. "What are you thinking?"

"I was thinking there might be an alternative to you regressing by moving back in with your folks." He side-eyes me. "What if you moved in with me?"

My heart flutters fast enough that I have to touch a hand to my chest like that will do something to calm it down. "Really? You're not only asking because my parents are shacking up together?"

"Boy, you're such a romantic." He snickers, then shakes his head. "No, I'm not only asking because your parents are shacking up together. Clearly, this has been on my mind, and you've given me the perfect opportunity to pop the question, so to speak."

Moving in together. When I check in with myself, there isn't so much as a hint of hesitation. My legendary instincts give me no reason to doubt this is the logical next step. Better than that. It's the next step I didn't know who wanted so badly until it was laid out in front of me.

"Yes," I whisper, unable to bite back a cheesy smile. "Yes, I would like to move in with you."

He doesn't say anything. He doesn't have to. It's enough for him to reach over and take my hand, which he holds the rest of the way to the restaurant.

In the middle of so much confusion and stress, his touch has the power to calm the noise in my head.

We pass the rest of the drive making plans, talking through ideas. Looking forward to the future.

ALEXIS

I can't remember the last time I was here.

Now, sitting outside the exquisite wrought iron gate leading into Broken Hill Cemetery, I almost wish I hadn't made the drive. It's one thing to consider visiting your sister's grave for the first time in forever, but another to sit only a few hundred yards from where she was laid to rest.

I've never been a spiritual person – we weren't raised that way. I do, however, believe there's something more than our lives here on Earth. There must be. Otherwise, what was it all for? You don't spend years studying killers and sometimes witnessing the depravity of humanity without needing to believe there's something else. Something better.

Forest of Lies

I know Maddie is not in that coffin. What's left of her body, yes, but not her. Now that I think of it, that could be the reason why I need to believe in an afterlife. I don't want to believe Tyler killed my sister's spirit. He may have destroyed her body, but he didn't take her spirit.

All the same, something about the Pete McClintock case leaves me thinking of her even more than usual. It could be how close she and Pete were in age. It could be hearing Becky's heartbreaking shrieks when she knew it was really the end. That there was no more hope. That's the sort of sound a person never forgets, and I was already familiar with it.

I can't sit out here all day. Rather than allow myself to freeze, I start the car again and turn onto the freshly shoveled path leading through the open gates and into the cemetery. The coating of fresh, white powder adds to the bleak atmosphere, and I wonder as I roll slowly through how many snowfalls some of the older graves have borne.

In other words, my thoughts are pretty dark, something I try to shake off before coming to a stop. The facility has gone modern at least when it comes to their maps, and I was able to look up Maddie's location online before setting out. Good thing, since the presence of snow only makes everything look painfully similar. I can imagine a person getting lost out here and staying lost for a long time.

What is it about being here that has me so shaken? The question haunts me as I crunch as gently as I can through the snow, remembering in the back of my head the way Mom scolded us once while we were visiting a relative's grave. Don't step on the neighbors. I can still hear it, and I remember the way Maddie looked at me out of the corner of her eye and tried not to laugh.

My heart aches at the memory. I miss her. It's not often that I allow myself to miss her.

I hope wherever she is, she understands that I haven't avoided visiting because I didn't want to. Maddie always was understanding. She was an ideal big sister, even when she could have brushed me aside. Five years is a big age difference at that time in a kid's life, the difference between being a child and a young woman. She never rubbed it in my face. Never made me feel lesser.

As I approach her grave and the sleek, gray headstone that marks it, my heart is full of what matters. The good memories. The parts of her she left behind.

That is what sits at the forefront of my thoughts when I reach the grave – until I see what's sitting on top of Maddie's headstone.

The most perfect red rose, its color vibrant against the white powder dusting the stone.

Forest of Lies

Immediately, my head snaps up, my heart lodged in my throat. There is not so much as a single snowflake resting on the perfect, blood red petals. Even more startling is the folded paper resting beneath the flower. As carefully as I can, I lift the message—on card stock, plain but thick — by its corner, careful not to leave prints. It looks and feels familiar. He must have left it here this morning, if not minutes ago. The note isn't even damp.

My pulse is racing and a sick sensation churns in my stomach, but I force myself to open the card and read what is carefully printed inside. Big, block letters, painstakingly formed.

I'm always with you.

Understanding slams into me. At first, I can't move. I can barely breathe. He was here. He was right here, minutes ago for all I know. Looking down, I examine the snow around me and identify fresh prints leading from the opposite direction from which I came. Large, heavy soled. Belonging to a man. He rounded the headstone from behind and stood almost where I stand now. Everything in me wants me to jump back, to not even touch his footprints. I want nothing of him around me.

What started as a hummingbird fluttering in my chest changes to something heavier. Pounding like a large drum, a steady, ominous sort of beat. I study the trees in the distance, a pair of large monuments sitting before them. Is that where he's hiding? Is he watching me now? He had no way of knowing I was coming here, but then who's to say? He's already proven what a keen interest he takes in my life and my habits.

Let him see me standing here, holding his little gifts. Let him see he hasn't broken me. My head is high and my demeanor calm. Let him see and let him know. I am going to find him. I am going to catch him.

I am going to stop him before he hurts anybody else.

THANK for you reading Forest of Lies. Can't wait to find out what happens to Alexis next? **Grab Forest of Obsession now!**

Forest of Lies

Forensic psychologist and FBI agent Alexis Forrest is on the hunt for a serial killer who has been terrorizing New England for decades. Years ago, her teenage sister fell victim to this predator, but the wrong person was convicted and sent to prison and the real killer is still out there.

The eerie calm of Broken Hill, Alexis's hometown, is shattered when a string of brutal killings resurfaces, echoing the nightmare of her past.

For years, everyone thought he was gone and then he strikes again.

After her father's house is burned down and her mother receives threats, Alexis knows she's running out of time.

The killer has set his sights on her.

With her own life on the line, she must confront her deepest fears in order to uncover the true identity of the illusive murderer before it's too late.

Teaming up once again with her former flame and partner, Mitch, Alexis plunges into a desperate race against time. But as the body count rises and the killer's taunts grow bolder, Alexis realizes she's facing someone who knows her every move.

With each step bringing her closer into the killer's twisted game, Alexis grapples with the chilling realization that the key to stopping the bloodshed may lie in the darkest corners of her own past.

Can she stop him in time or will she become just another one of his victims?

1-click Forest of Obsession now!

IF YOU ENJOYED THIS BOOK, please don't forget to leave a review on Amazon and Goodreads! Reviews help me find new readers.

If you have any issues with anything in the book or find any typos, please email me at Kate@kategable.com. Thank you so much for reading!

. . .

Forest of Lies

ALSO CHECK out my other bestselling and 3 time Silver Falchion award winning series, **Girl Missing.**

When her 13-year-old sister vanishes on her way back from a friend's house, Detective Kaitlyn Carr must confront demons from her own past in order to bring her sister home.

The small mountain town of Big Bear Lake is only three hours away but a world away from her life in Los Angeles. It's the place she grew up and the place that's plagued her with lies, death and secrets.

As Kaitlyn digs deeper into the murder that she is investigating and her sister's disappearance, she finds out that appearances are misleading and few things are what they seem.

A murderer is lurking in the shadows and the more of the mystery that Kaitlyn unspools the closer she gets to danger herself.

Can Kaitlyn find the killer and solve the mystery of her sister's disappearance before it's too late?

What happens when someone else is taken?

1-click Girl Missing now!

ABOUT KATE GABLE

Kate Gable loves a good mystery that is full of suspense. She grew up devouring psychological thrillers and crime novels as well as movies, tv shows and true crime.

Her favorite stories are the ones that are centered on families with lots of secrets and lies as well as many twists and turns. Her novels have elements of psychological suspense, thriller, mystery and romance.

Kate Gable lives near Palm Springs, CA with her husband, son, a dog and a cat. She has spent more than twenty years in Southern California and finds inspiration from its cities, canyons, deserts, and small mountain towns.

She graduated from University of Southern California with a Bachelor's degree in Mathematics. After pursuing graduate studies in mathematics, she switched gears and got her MA in Creative Writing and English from Western New Mexico University and her PhD in Education from Old Dominion University.

Writing has always been her passion and obsession. Kate is also a USA Today Bestselling author of romantic suspense under another pen name.

Write her here:

Kate@kategable.com

Check out her books here:

www.kategable.com

Sign up for my newsletter:
https://www.subscribepage.com/kategableviplist

Join my Facebook Group:
https://www.facebook.com/groups/833851020557518

Bonus Points: Follow me on BookBub and Goodreads!

https://www.bookbub.com/authors/kate-gable

https://www.goodreads.com/author/show/21534224.Kate_Gable

- amazon.com/Kate-Gable/e/B095XFCLL7
- facebook.com/KateGableAuthor
- bookbub.com/authors/kate-gable
- instagram.com/kategablebooks
- tiktok.com/@kategablebooks

ALSO BY KATE GABLE

Detective Kaitlyn Carr Psychological Mystery series
Girl Missing (Book 1)
Girl Lost (Book 2)
Girl Found (Book 3)
Girl Taken (Book 4)
Girl Forgotten (Book 5)
Gone Too Soon (Book 6)
Gone Forever (Book 7)
Whispers in the Sand (Book 8)

Girl Hidden (FREE Novella)

Detective Charlotte Pierce Psychological Mystery series
Last Breath
Nameless Girl

Missing Lives
Girl in the Lake